DEAD MAN'S FOLLY

THE AGATHA CHRISTIE COLLECTION

Mysteries

The Man in the Brown
  Suit
The Secret of Chimneys
The Seven Dials Mystery
The Mysterious Mr Quin
The Sittaford Mystery
The Hound of Death
The Listerdale Mystery
Why Didn't They Ask
  Evans?
Parker Pyne Investigates
Murder Is Easy
And Then There Were
  None
Towards Zero
Death Comes as the End
Sparkling Cyanide
Crooked House
They Came to Baghdad
Destination Unknown
Spider's Web*
The Unexpected Guest*
Ordeal by Innocence
The Pale Horse
Endless Night
Passenger To Frankfurt
Problem at Pollensa Bay
While the Light Lasts

Poirot

The Mysterious Affair at
  Styles
The Murder on the
  Links
Poirot Investigates
The Murder of Roger
  Ackroyd
The Big Four
The Mystery of the Blue
  Train
Black Coffee*
Peril at End House
Lord Edgware Dies

Murder on the Orient
  Express
Three Act Tragedy
Death in the Clouds
The ABC Murders
Murder in Mesopotamia
Cards on the Table
Murder in the Mews
Dumb Witness
Death on the Nile
Appointment With Death
Hercule Poirot's
  Christmas
Sad Cypress
One, Two, Buckle My Shoe
Evil Under the Sun
Five Little Pigs
The Hollow
The Labours of
  Hercules
Taken at the Flood
Mrs McGinty's Dead
After the Funeral
Hickory Dickory Dock
Dead Man's Folly
Cat Among the Pigeons
The Adventure of the
  Christmas Pudding
The Clocks
Third Girl
Hallowe'en Party
Elephants Can
  Remember
Poirot's Early Cases
Curtain: Poirot's Last
  Case

Marple

The Murder at the
  Vicarage
The Thirteen Problems
The Body in the Library
The Moving Finger
A Murder Is Announced

They Do It With Mirrors
A Pocket Full of Rye
4.50 from Paddington
The Mirror Crack'd from
  Side to Side
A Caribbean Mystery
At Bertram's Hotel
Nemesis
Sleeping Murder
Miss Marple's Final
  Cases

Tommy & Tuppence

The Secret Adversary
Partners in Crime
N or M?
By the Pricking of My
  Thumbs
Postern of Fate

Published as Mary
  Westmacott

Giant's Bread
Unfinished Portrait
Absent in the Spring
The Rose and the Yew
  Tree
A Daughter's a
  Daughter
The Burden

Memoirs

An Autobiography
Come, Tell Me How You
  Live
The Grand Tour

Plays and Stories

Akhnaton
The Mousetrap and
  Other Plays
The Floating Admiral
  (contributor)
Star Over Bethlehem

* novelized by Charles Osborne

Agatha Christie

Dead Man's Folly

HARPER

HARPER

An imprint of HarperCollins*Publishers*
77–85 Fulham Palace Road,
Hammersmith, London W6 8JB
www.harpercollins.co.uk

This paperback edition 2014

First published in Great Britain by
Collins 1956

A catalogue record for this book is
available from the British Library

ISBN 978-0-00-755687-8

Set in Sabon by Palimpsest Book Production Ltd.,
Falkirk, Stirlingshire

Printed and bound in Great Britain by
Clays Ltd, St Ives plc

MIX
Paper from
responsible sources
FSC **FSC® C007454**
www.fsc.org

FSC™ is a non-profit international organisation established to promote
the responsible management of the world's forests. Products carrying the
FSC label are independently certified to assure consumers that they come
from forests that are managed to meet the social, economic and
ecological needs of present and future generations,
and other controlled sources.

Find out more about HarperCollins and the environment at
www.harpercollins.co.uk/green

To Peggy and Humphrey Trevelyan

DEAD MAN'S FOLLY:
AN INTRODUCTION

by Mathew Prichard

Unusually for Agatha Christie, *Dead Man's Folly* was written around a specific location, in this case Greenway House on the River Dart in South Devon. Greenway was where Nima (which is what I called my grandmother) used to spend her summer holidays almost from the time she bought it in 1938 until she died in 1976. And it seems appropriate to be celebrating this fact in 2014 with a reissue of *Dead Man's Folly*, as it is now 15 years since Greenway was acquired by the National Trust and subsequently opened to the public.

But last year something even more momentous happened at Greenway. ITV's series *Agatha Christie's Poirot* starring David Suchet shot its final film there, *Dead Man's Folly*, and so a series that had begun in 1989 with *The Adventure of the Clapham Cook* ended in a blaze of glory at Greenway itself. Neither Nima, nor my late mother Rosalind, who had a lot to do with setting up the TV series in the beginning, could have wished for anything better. It was as if Hercule Poirot had come home.

As luck would have it, we were blessed with wonderful summer weather, and the last day of shooting in front of the house—a scene that was not in itself dramatically very significant—was none the less poignant as it featured David Suchet, in full Poirot regalia, mincing up Greenway's front steps in his own inimitable way and knocking on the door. Eventually, after three repeats of the same action, we heard the time-honoured words—'it's a wrap'—and there was not a dry eye in the house, or rather on the lawn, where a large crowd had come to celebrate the ending of one of the world's best loved TV series, and the portrayal of one of our best loved literary characters, Hercule Poirot, by one of our best loved character actors, David Suchet. If anyone had told Nima (who sadly never met David Suchet) that a series of this magnitude and popularity would be made continuously over a period of 25 years, I am sure that she would not have believed it.

My particular affection for *Dead Man's Folly* extends back to long before the filming of the TV series, though. The book was published in 1956, when I was 13, coinciding with both the time I was beginning to enjoy reading Nima's books, and when as a schoolboy I spent my summer holidays at Greenway with my family including, of course, Nima. I cannot say that I ever remember a fête on the lawn, but I certainly remember smaller events there, as Greenway was host to an ever-growing selection of literary and theatrical friends (this was the heyday of Nima's career as a

West End playwright), with plenty of friends of my step-grandfather Max Mallowan from the world of archaeology added for good measure. Nima never based her characters entirely on real-life people, but I would be lying if I did not admit to recognizing snippets of Sir George and Lady Stubbs, and particularly Mrs Folliatt, from actual people whom she knew. Nor was I surprised when I found out that *Dead Man's Folly* featured hitch-hikers. We were familiar with the occasional hitch-hiker from the nearby youth hostel called Maypool.

But I suppose *Dead Man's Folly* evokes two particular memories from my childhood that I find particularly poignant: one a person, one a place. The person is Ariadne Oliver, who, although rather more boisterous than Nima would ever be, did have something of her enthusiasm, her love of apples, and a writer's curiosity that reminds me very much of Nima herself. She appeared in seven novels, six of them with Poirot, and Zoë Wanamaker gives an excellent performance in the film. The place is the boathouse, where the poor victim is found murdered. Nima and I used to walk down to Greenway's boathouse in the afternoon, watch the pleasure cruisers sail by (the *Kiloran*, *Pride of Paignton*, *Brixham Belle* and those wonderful paddle streamers, one of which I am delighted to say is still in working order). The tour guides on these boats would always refer to Greenway, usually inaccurately, as the home of Agatha Christie (rather than, strictly speaking, her holiday home), and though we could hear their voices as they sailed past, never do I remember them actually recognizing her as she sat inconspicuously in the boathouse with her grandson!

As I read the book again now, I do seem to remember reading it originally on publication as a young teenager and understanding perhaps for the first time a little more about the construction of a detective story in relation to real people and real places, because I was familiar with those in this particular book. This authenticity is of course one of the reasons why Nima's books still seem so real and convincing today. Back then, the books based around archaeology and the Middle East were pure fiction to me, although Nima used exactly the same techniques, drawing on characteristics of real people and factual landmarks and adding a fictional dimension, just as she did with *Dead Man's Folly*. I hope one day that I will be able to visit Nimrud, the Pyramids in Egypt, or some other locations which inspired Nima, so that I can see them as she did. I recently visited one specific place of inspiration in Tenerife in the Canary Islands, the setting for a Harley Quin story called 'The Man from the Sea' (in the book *The Mysterious Mr Quin*)—it is a brilliant short story, and all the better for having been there.

One other family reminiscence concerning *Dead Man's Folly* concerns its literary origins. *Dead Man's Folly* is a longer, expanded version of a short story called 'The Greenshore Folly'. Originally, Nima offered the royalties from the short story to the Diocese of Exeter to help pay for stained glass windows in her local church at Churston, near Greenway. Unfortunately, her agent could not sell the story to one of the usual magazines that printed them because it was longer than her normal short stories, and the Diocese grew impatient, as by then it had committed to buy the windows! In the end, Nima wrote a shorter story for the Diocese entitled 'Greenshaw's Folly' (featuring Miss Marple rather than Poirot), and decided to lengthen 'The Greenshore Folly' and publish it as a full-length book, *Dead Man's Folly*. So, in the end everybody got what they needed, and if you visit Greenway do pay a visit to Churston Church, as the windows are magnificent. (And if you are interested in the original 1954 shorter version of the Folly, *Hercule Poirot and the Greenshore Folly* is also being published in 2014 to mark its Diamond Anniversary.)

As you probably know, my family gave Greenway to the National Trust in 1999 and it is open to the public for most of the year. Everyone can now visit the boathouse where the murder took place, or relax on a chair near where Hattie Stubbs sat and be polite to the hikers who are now allowed to enter the grounds! You may also find that the National Trust shop has the finest collection of Agatha Christie books in the West of England. Though *Dead Man's Folly* is unusual in being so closely based on a real place, it is not the only Agatha Christie book that has echoes of Greenway. If you enjoy it, you should certainly read *Five Little Pigs* as well, with a murder on Greenway's Battery!

Finally, one of the words I have often chosen to describe Agatha Christie's books and films is 'welcoming', and I do think that Robyn Brown and Gary Calland, the two General

Agatha Christie

Managers the Trust has employed since 1999, and all their staff, have surpassed themselves in making Greenway as welcoming a place as Nima did when I was young. I hope that having read *Dead Man's Folly*, and maybe watched the film with David Suchet, that you can visit the original location. What a treat you have in store!

CHAPTER 1

It was Miss Lemon, Poirot's efficient secretary, who took the telephone call.

Laying aside her shorthand notebook, she raised the receiver and said without emphasis, 'Trafalgar 8137.'

Hercule Poirot leaned back in his upright chair and closed his eyes. His fingers beat a meditative soft tattoo on the edge of the table. In his head he continued to compose the polished periods of the letter he had been dictating.

Placing her hand over the receiver, Miss Lemon asked in a low voice:

'Will you accept a personal call from Nassecombe, Devon?'

Poirot frowned. The place meant nothing to him.

'The name of the caller?' he demanded cautiously.

Miss Lemon spoke into the mouthpiece.

'*Air-raid?*' she asked doubtingly. 'Oh, yes—what was the last name again?'

Once more she turned to Hercule Poirot.

Agatha Christie

'Mrs Ariadne Oliver.'

Hercule Poirot's eyebrows shot up. A memory rose in his mind: windswept grey hair... an eagle profile...

He rose and replaced Miss Lemon at the telephone.

'Hercule Poirot speaks,' he announced grandiloquently.

'Is that Mr Hercules Porrot speaking personally?' the suspicious voice of the telephone operator demanded.

Poirot assured her that that was the case.

'You're through to Mr Porrot,' said the voice.

Its thin reedy accents were replaced by a magnificent booming contralto which caused Poirot hastily to shift the receiver a couple of inches farther from his ear.

'M. Poirot, is that really *you*?' demanded Mrs Oliver.

'Myself in person, Madame.'

'This is Mrs Oliver. I don't know if you'll remember me—'

'But of course I remember you, Madame. Who could forget you?'

'Well, people do sometimes,' said Mrs Oliver. 'Quite often, in fact. I don't think that I've got a very distinctive personality. Or perhaps it's because I'm always doing different things to my hair. But all that's neither here nor there. I hope I'm not interrupting you when you're frightfully busy?'

'No, no, you do not derange me in the least.'

'Good gracious—I'm sure I don't want to drive you out of your mind. The fact is, I *need* you.'

'Need me?'

'Yes, at once. Can you take an aeroplane?'

'I do not take aeroplanes. They make me sick.'

2

'They do me, too. Anyway, I don't suppose it would be any quicker than the train really, because I think the only airport near here is Exeter which is miles away. So come by train. Twelve o'clock from Paddington to Nassecombe. You can do it nicely. You've got three-quarters of an hour if my watch is right—though it isn't usually.'

'But where are you, Madame? What is all this *about*?'

'Nasse House, Nassecombe. A car or taxi will meet you at the station at Nassecombe.'

'But why do you need me? What is all this *about*?' Poirot repeated frantically.

'Telephones are in such awkward places,' said Mrs Oliver. 'This one's in the hall... People passing through and talking... I can't really hear. But I'm expecting you. Everybody will be *so* thrilled. Goodbye.'

There was a sharp click as the receiver was replaced. The line hummed gently.

With a baffled air of bewilderment, Poirot put back the receiver and murmured something under his breath. Miss Lemon sat with her pencil poised, incurious. She repeated in muted tones the final phrase of dictation before the interruption.

'—allow me to assure you, my dear sir, that the hypothesis you have advanced...'

Poirot waved aside the advancement of the hypothesis.

'That was Mrs Oliver,' he said. 'Ariadne Oliver, the detective novelist. You may have read...' But he stopped, remembering that Miss Lemon only read improving books and regarded such frivolities as fictional crime with contempt. 'She wants me to go down to Devonshire today, at once, in'—he glanced at the clock—'thirty-five minutes.'

Miss Lemon raised disapproving eyebrows.

'That will be running it rather fine,' she said. 'For what reason?'

'You may well ask! She did not tell me.'

'How very peculiar. Why not?'

'Because,' said Hercule Poirot thoughtfully, 'she was afraid of being overheard. Yes, she made that quite clear.'

'Well, really,' said Miss Lemon, bristling in her employer's defence. 'The things people expect! Fancy thinking that you'd go rushing off on some wild goose chase like that! An important man like you! I have always noticed that these artists and writers are very unbalanced—no sense of propor-tion. Shall I telephone through a telegram: *Regret unable leave London?*'

Her hand went out to the telephone. Poirot's voice arrested the gesture.

'*Du tout!*' he said. 'On the contrary. Be so kind as to summon a taxi immediately.' He raised his voice. 'Georges! A few necessities of toilet in my small valise. And quickly, very quickly, I have a train to catch.'

II

The train, having done one hundred and eighty-odd miles of its two hundred and twelve miles journey at top speed, puffed gently and apologetically through the last thirty and drew into Nassecombe station. Only one person alighted, Hercule Poirot. He negotiated with care a yawning gap between the step of the train and the platform and looked round him. At the far end of the train a porter was busy inside a luggage compartment. Poirot picked up his valise and walked back along the platform to the exit. He gave up his ticket and walked out through the booking-office.

A large Humber saloon was drawn up outside and a chauffeur in uniform came forward.

'Mr Hercule Poirot?' he inquired respectfully.

He took Poirot's case from him and opened the door of the car. They drove away from the station over the railway bridge and turned down a country lane which wound between high hedges on either side. Presently the ground fell away on the right and disclosed a very beautiful river view with hills of a misty blue in the distance. The chauffeur drew into the hedge and stopped.

'The River Helm, sir,' he said. 'With Dartmoor in the distance.'

It was clear that admiration was necessary. Poirot made the necessary noises, murmuring *Magnifique!* several times. Actually, Nature appealed to him very little. A well-cultivated neatly arranged kitchen garden was far more likely to bring a murmur of admiration to Poirot's lips. Two girls passed the car, toiling slowly up the hill. They were carrying heavy rucksacks on their backs and wore shorts, with bright coloured scarves tied over their heads.

'There is a Youth Hostel next door to us, sir,' explained the chauffeur, who had clearly constituted himself Poirot's guide to Devon. 'Hoodown Park. Mr Fletcher's place it used to be. The Youth Hostel Association bought it and it's fairly crammed in summer time. Take in over a hundred a night, they do. They're not allowed to stay longer than a couple of nights—then they've got to move on. Both sexes and mostly foreigners.'

Poirot nodded absently. He was reflecting, not for the first time, that seen from the back, shorts were becoming to very few of the female sex. He shut his eyes in pain. Why, oh why, must young women array themselves thus? Those scarlet thighs were singularly unattractive!

'They seem heavily laden,' he murmured.

'Yes, sir, and it's a long pull from the station or the bus stop. Best part of two miles to Hoodown Park.' He hesitated. 'If you don't object, sir, we could give them a lift?'

'By all means, by all means,' said Poirot benignantly. There was he in luxury in an almost empty car and here were these two panting and perspiring young women weighed down with heavy rucksacks and without the least idea how to dress themselves so as to appear attractive to the other sex. The chauffeur started the car and came to a slow purring halt beside the two girls. Their flushed and perspiring faces were raised hopefully.

Poirot opened the door and the girls climbed in.

'It is most kind, please,' said one of them, a fair girl with a foreign accent. 'It is longer way than I think, yes.'

The other girl, who had a sunburnt and deeply flushed face with bronzed chestnut curls peeping out beneath her headscarf, merely nodded her head several times, flashed her teeth, and murmured, *Grazie*. The fair girl continued to talk vivaciously.

'I to England come for two week holiday. I come from Holland. I like England very much. I have been Stratford Avon, Shakespeare Theatre and Warwick Castle. Then I have been Clovelly, now I have seen Exeter Cathedral and Torquay—very nice—I come to famous beauty spot here and tomorrow I cross river, go to Plymouth where discovery of New World was made from Plymouth Hoe.'

'And you, signorina?' Poirot turned to the other girl. But she only smiled and shook her curls.

'She does not much English speak,' said the Dutch girl kindly. 'We both a little French speak—so we talk in train. She is coming from near Milan and has relative in England married to gentleman who keeps shop for much groceries. She has come with friend to Exeter yesterday, but friend has eat veal ham pie not good from shop in Exeter and has to stay there sick. It is not good in hot weather, the veal ham pie.'

At this point the chauffeur slowed down where the road forked. The girls got out, uttered thanks in two languages and proceeded up the left-hand road. The chauffeur laid aside for a moment his Olympian aloofness and said feelingly to Poirot:

'It's not only veal and ham pie—you want to be careful of Cornish pasties too. Put *anything* in a pasty they will, holiday time!'

He restarted the car and drove down the right-hand road which shortly afterwards passed into thick woods. He proceeded to give a final verdict on the occupants of Hoodown Park Youth Hostel.

'Nice enough young women, some of 'em, at that hostel,' he said; 'but it's hard to get them to understand about trespassing. Absolutely shocking the way they trespass. Don't seem to understand that a gentleman's place is *private* here. Always coming through our woods, they are, and pretending that they don't understand what you say to them.' He shook his head darkly.

They went on, down a steep hill through woods, then through big iron gates, and along a drive, winding up finally in front of a big white Georgian house looking out over the river.

The chauffeur opened the door of the car as a tall black-haired butler appeared on the steps.

'Mr Hercule Poirot?' murmured the latter.

'Yes.'

'Mrs Oliver is expecting you, sir. You will find her down at the Battery. Allow me to show you the way.'

Poirot was directed to a winding path that led along the wood with glimpses of the river below. The path descended gradually until it came out at last on an open space, round in shape, with a low battlemented parapet. On the parapet Mrs Oliver was sitting.

She rose to meet him and several apples fell from her lap and rolled in all directions. Apples seemed to be an inescapable *motif* of meeting Mrs Oliver.

'I can't think why I always drop things,' said Mrs Oliver

somewhat indistinctly, since her mouth was full of apple. 'How are you, M. Poirot?'

'*Très bien, chère Madame,*' replied Poirot politely. 'And you?'

Mrs Oliver was looking somewhat different from when Poirot had last seen her, and the reason lay, as she had already hinted over the telephone, in the fact that she had once more experimented with her *coiffure*. The last time Poirot had seen her, she had been adopting a wind-swept effect. Today, her hair, richly blued, was piled upward in a multiplicity of rather artificial little curls in a pseudo Marquise style. The Marquise effect ended at her neck; the rest of her could have been definitely labelled 'country practical,' consisting of a violent yolk-of-egg rough tweed coat and skirt and a rather bilious-looking mustard-coloured jumper.

'I knew you'd come,' said Mrs Oliver cheerfully.

'You could not possibly have known,' said Poirot severely.

'Oh, yes, I did.'

'I still ask myself *why* I am here.'

'Well, I know the answer. Curiosity.'

Poirot looked at her and his eyes twinkled a little. 'Your famous woman's intuition,' he said, 'has, perhaps, for once not led you too far astray.'

'Now, don't laugh at my woman's intuition. Haven't I always spotted the murderer right away?'

Poirot was gallantly silent. Otherwise he might have replied, 'At the fifth attempt, perhaps, and not always then!'

Instead he said, looking round him:

'It is indeed a beautiful property that you have here.'

'This? But it doesn't belong to *me*, M. Poirot. Did you think it did? Oh, no, it belongs to some people called Stubbs.'

'Who are they?'

'Oh, nobody really,' said Mrs Oliver vaguely. 'Just rich. No, I'm down here professionally, doing a job.'

'Ah, you are getting local colour for one of your *chefs-d'oeuvre*?'

'No, no. Just what I said. I'm doing a *job*. I've been engaged to arrange a murder.'

Poirot stared at her.

'Oh, not a real one,' said Mrs Oliver reassuringly. 'There's a big fête thing on tomorrow, and as a kind of novelty there's going to be a Murder Hunt. Arranged by me. Like a Treasure Hunt, you see; only they've had a Treasure Hunt so often that they thought this would be a novelty. So they offered me a very substantial fee to come down and think it up. Quite fun, really—rather a change from the usual grim routine.'

'How does it work?'

'Well, there'll be a Victim, of course. And Clues. And Suspects. All rather conventional—you know, the Vamp and the Blackmailer and the Young Lovers and the Sinister Butler and so on. Half a crown to enter and you get shown the first Clue and you've got to find the Victim, and the Weapon and say Whodunnit and the Motive. And there are Prizes.'

'Remarkable!' said Hercule Poirot.

'Actually,' said Mrs Oliver ruefully, 'it's all much harder to arrange than you'd think. Because you've got to allow for real people being quite intelligent, and in my books they needn't be.'

'And it is to assist you in arranging this that you have sent for me?'

Poirot did not try very hard to keep an outraged resentment out of his voice.

'Oh, *no*,' said Mrs Oliver. 'Of course not! I've done all that. Everything's all set for tomorrow. No, I wanted you for quite another reason.'

'What reason?'

Mrs Oliver's hands strayed upward to her head. She was just about to sweep them frenziedly through her hair in the old familiar gesture when she remembered the intricacy of her hair-do. Instead, she relieved her feelings by tugging at her ear lobes.

'I dare say I'm a fool,' she said. 'But I think there's something wrong.'

CHAPTER 2

There was a moment's silence as Poirot stared at her. Then he asked sharply: 'Something *wrong*? How?'

'I don't know… That's what I want *you* to find out. But I've felt—more and more—that I was being—oh!—*engineered*… jockeyed along… Call me a fool if you like, but I can only say that if there was to be a *real* murder tomorrow instead of a fake one, I shouldn't be surprised!'

Poirot stared at her and she looked back at him defiantly.

'Very interesting,' said Poirot.

'I suppose you think I'm a complete fool,' said Mrs Oliver defensively.

'I have never thought you a fool,' said Poirot.

'And I know what you always say—or look—about intuition.'

'One calls things by different names,' said Poirot. 'I am quite ready to believe that you have noticed something, or heard something, that has definitely aroused in you anxiety. I think it is possible that you yourself may not even know just what

12

it is that you have seen or noticed or heard. You are aware only of the *result*. If I may so put it, you do not know what it is that you know. You may label that intuition if you like.'

'It makes one feel such a fool,' said Mrs Oliver, ruefully, 'not to be able to be *definite*.'

'We shall arrive,' said Poirot encouragingly. 'You say that you have had the feeling of being—how did you put it— jockeyed along? Can you explain a little more clearly what you mean by that?'

'Well, it's rather difficult... You see, this is *my* murder, so to speak. I've thought it out and planned it and it all fits in—dovetails. Well, if you know anything at all about writers, you'll know that they can't stand suggestions. People say "Splendid, but wouldn't it be better if so and so did so and so?" or "Wouldn't it be a wonderful idea if the victim was A instead of B? Or the murderer turned out to be D instead of E?" I mean, one wants to say: "All right then, write it yourself if you want it that way!"'

Poirot nodded.

'And that is what has been happening?'

'Not quite... That sort of silly suggestion has been made, and then I've flared up, and they've given in, but have just slipped in some quite minor trivial suggestion and because I've made a stand over the other, I've accepted the triviality without noticing much.'

'I see,' said Poirot. 'Yes—it is a method, that... Something rather crude and preposterous is put forward—but that is not really the point. The small minor alteration is really the objective. Is that what you mean?'

Agatha Christie

'That's exactly what I mean,' said Mrs Oliver. 'And, of course, I *may* be imagining it, but I don't think I am—and none of the things seem to matter anyway. But it's got me worried—that, and a sort of—well—*atmosphere*.'

'Who has made these suggestions of alterations to you?'

'Different people,' said Mrs Oliver. 'If it was just *one* person I'd be more sure of my ground. But it's not just one person—although I think it is really. I mean it's one person working through other quite unsuspecting people.'

'Have you an idea as to who that one person is?'

Mrs Oliver shook her head.

'It's somebody very clever and very careful,' she said. 'It might be anybody.'

'Who is there?' asked Poirot. 'The cast of characters must be fairly limited?'

'Well,' began Mrs Oliver. 'There's Sir George Stubbs who owns this place. Rich and plebeian and frightfully stupid outside business, I should think, but probably dead sharp in it. And there's Lady Stubbs—Hattie—about twenty years younger than he is, rather beautiful, but dumb as a fish—in fact, I think she's definitely halfwitted. Married him for his money, of course, and doesn't think about anything but clothes and jewels. Then there's Michael Weyman—he's an architect, quite young, and good-looking in a craggy kind of artistic way. He's designing a tennis pavilion for Sir George and repairing the Folly.'

'Folly? What is that—a masquerade?'

'No, it's architectural. One of those little sort of temple things, white, with columns. You've probably seen them at Kew. Then there's Miss Brewis, she's a sort of secretary

14

housekeeper, who runs things and writes letters—very grim and efficient. And then there are the people round about who come in and help. A young married couple who have taken a cottage down by the river—Alec Legge and his wife Sally. And Captain Warburton, who's the Mastertons' agent. And the Mastertons, of course, and old Mrs Folliat who lives in what used to be the lodge. Her husband's people owned Nasse originally. But they've died out, or been killed in wars, and there were lots of death duties so the last heir sold the place.'

Poirot considered this list of characters, but at the moment they were only names to him. He returned to the main issue.

'Whose idea was the Murder Hunt?'

'Mrs Masterton's, I think. She's the local M.P.'s wife, very good at organizing. It was she who persuaded Sir George to have the fête here. You see the place has been empty for so many years that she thinks people will be keen to pay and come in to see it.'

'That all seems straightforward enough,' said Poirot.

'It all *seems* straightforward,' said Mrs Oliver obstinately; 'but it isn't. I tell you, M. Poirot, there's something *wrong*.'

Poirot looked at Mrs Oliver and Mrs Oliver looked back at Poirot.

'How have you accounted for my presence here? For your summons to me?' Poirot asked.

'That was easy,' said Mrs Oliver. 'You're to give away the prizes for the Murder Hunt. Everybody's awfully thrilled. I said I knew you, and could probably persuade you to come and that I was sure your name would be a terrific draw—as, of course, it will be,' Mrs Oliver added tactfully.

'And the suggestion was accepted—without demur?'

'I tell you, everybody was thrilled.'

Mrs Oliver thought it unnecessary to mention that amongst the younger generation one or two had asked 'Who *is* Hercule Poirot?'

'*Everybody?* Nobody spoke against the idea?'

Mrs Oliver shook her head.

'That is a pity,' said Hercule Poirot.

'You mean it might have given us a line?'

'A would-be criminal could hardly be expected to welcome my presence.'

'I suppose you think I've imagined the whole thing,' said Mrs Oliver ruefully. 'I must admit that until I started talking to you I hadn't realized how very little I've got to go upon.'

'Calm yourself,' said Poirot kindly. 'I am intrigued and interested. Where do we begin?'

Mrs Oliver glanced at her watch.

'It's just tea-time. We'll go back to the house and then you can meet everybody.'

She took a different path from the one by which Poirot had come. This one seemed to lead in the opposite direction.

'We pass by the boathouse this way,' Mrs Oliver explained.

As she spoke the boathouse came into view. It jutted out on to the river and was a picturesque thatched affair.

'That's where the Body's going to be,' said Mrs Oliver. 'The body for the Murder Hunt, I mean.'

'And who is going to be killed?'

'Oh, a girl hiker, who is really the Yugoslavian first wife of a young Atom Scientist,' said Mrs Oliver glibly.

Poirot blinked.

'Of course it looks as though the Atom Scientist had killed her—but naturally it's not as simple as that.'

'Naturally not—since *you* are concerned…'

Mrs Oliver accepted the compliment with a wave of the hand.

'Actually,' she said, 'she's killed by the Country Squire—and the motive is really rather ingenious—I don't believe many people will get it—though there's a perfectly clear pointer in the fifth clue.'

Poirot abandoned the subtleties of Mrs Oliver's plot to ask a practical question:

'But how do you arrange for a suitable body?'

'Girl Guide,' said Mrs Oliver. 'Sally Legge was going to be it—but now they want her to dress up in a turban and do the fortune telling. So it's a Girl Guide called Marlene Tucker. Rather dumb and sniffs,' she added in an explanatory manner. 'It's quite easy—just peasant scarves and a rucksack—and all she has to do when she hears someone coming is to flop down on the floor and arrange the cord round her neck. Rather dull for the poor kid—just sticking inside that boathouse until she's found, but I've arranged for her to have a nice bundle of comics—there's a clue to the murderer scribbled on one of them as a matter of fact—so it all works in.'

'Your ingenuity leaves me spellbound! The things you think of!'

'It's never difficult to *think* of things,' said Mrs Oliver.

'The trouble is that you think of too many, and then it all becomes too complicated, so you have to relinquish some of them and that *is* rather agony. We go up this way now.'

They started up a steep zig-zagging path that led them back along the river at a higher level. At a twist through the trees they came out on a space surmounted by a small white pilastered temple. Standing back and frowning at it was a young man wearing dilapidated flannel trousers and a shirt of rather virulent green. He spun round towards them.

'Mr Michael Weyman, M. Hercule Poirot,' said Mrs Oliver.

The young man acknowledged the introduction with a careless nod.

'Extraordinary,' he said bitterly, 'the places people *put* things! This thing here, for instance. Put up only about a year ago—quite nice of its kind and quite in keeping with the period of the house. But why *here*? These things were meant to be seen—"situated on an eminence"—that's how they phrased it—with a nice grassy approach and daffodils, et cetera. But here's this poor little devil, stuck away in the midst of trees—not visible from anywhere—you'd have to cut down about twenty trees before you'd even see it from the river.'

'Perhaps there wasn't any other place,' said Mrs Oliver.

Michael Weyman snorted.

'Top of that grassy bank by the house—perfect natural setting. But no, these tycoon fellows are all the same—no artistic sense. Has a fancy for a "Folly," as he calls it, orders one. Looks round for somewhere to put it. Then, I understand, a big oak tree crashes down in a gale. Leaves a nasty scar. "Oh, we'll tidy the place up by putting a Folly there," says the silly ass. That's all they ever think about, these rich city fellows, tidying up! I wonder he hasn't put beds of red geraniums and calceolarias all round the house! A man like that shouldn't be allowed to own a place like this!'

He sounded heated.

'This young man,' Poirot observed to himself, 'assuredly does not like Sir George Stubbs.'

'It's bedded down in concrete,' said Weyman. 'And there's loose soil underneath—so it's subsided. Cracked all up here— it will be dangerous soon… Better pull the whole thing down and re-erect it on the top of the bank near the house. That's my advice, but the obstinate old fool won't hear of it.'

'What about the tennis pavilion?' asked Mrs Oliver.

Gloom settled even more deeply on the young man.

'He wants a kind of Chinese pagoda,' he said, with a groan. 'Dragons if you please! Just because Lady Stubbs fancies herself in Chinese coolie hats. Who'd be an architect? Anyone who wants something decent built hasn't got the money, and those who have the money want something too utterly goddam awful!'

'You have my commiserations,' said Poirot gravely.

'George Stubbs,' said the architect scornfully. 'Who does he think he is? Dug himself into some cushy Admiralty job in the safe depths of Wales during the war—and grows a beard to suggest he saw active naval service on convoy duty—or that's what they say. Stinking with money—absolutely stinking!'

'Well, you architects have got to have someone who's got money to spend, or you'd never have a job,' Mrs Oliver pointed out reasonably enough. She moved on towards the house and Poirot and the dispirited architect prepared to follow her.

'These tycoons,' said the latter bitterly, 'can't understand first principles.' He delivered a final kick to the lopsided Folly. 'If the foundations are rotten—everything's rotten.'

'It is profound what you say there,' said Poirot. 'Yes, it is profound.'

The path they were following came out from the trees and the house showed white and beautiful before them in its setting of dark trees rising up behind it.

'It is of a veritable beauty, yes,' murmured Poirot.

'He wants to build a billiard room on,' said Mr Weyman venomously.

On the bank below them a small elderly lady was busy with secateurs on a clump of shrubs. She climbed up to greet them, panting slightly.

'Everything neglected for years,' she said. 'And so difficult nowadays to get a man who understands shrubs. This hillside should be a blaze of colour in March and April, but very disappointing this year—all this dead wood ought to have been cut away last autumn—'

'M. Hercule Poirot, Mrs Folliat,' said Mrs Oliver.

The elderly lady beamed.

'So this is the great M. Poirot! It *is* kind of you to come and help us tomorrow. This clever lady here has thought out a most puzzling problem—it will be such a novelty.'

Poirot was faintly puzzled by the graciousness of the little lady's manner. She might, he thought, have been his hostess.

He said politely:

'Mrs Oliver is an old friend of mine. I was delighted to be able to respond to her request. This is indeed a beautiful spot, and what a superb and noble mansion.'

Mrs Folliat nodded in a matter-of-fact manner.

'Yes. It was built by my husband's great-grandfather in 1790. There was an Elizabethan house previously. It fell into disrepair and burned down in about 1700. Our family has lived here since 1598.'

Her voice was calm and matter of fact. Poirot looked at her with closer attention. He saw a very small and compact little person, dressed in shabby tweeds. The most noticeable feature about her was her clear china-blue eyes. Her grey hair was closely confined by a hairnet. Though obviously careless of her appearance, she had that indefinable air of being someone which is so hard to explain.

As they walked together towards the house, Poirot said diffidently, 'It must be hard for you to have strangers living here.'

There was a moment's pause before Mrs Folliat answered. Her voice was clear and precise and curiously devoid of emotion.

'So many things are hard, M. Poirot,' she said.

CHAPTER 3

It was Mrs Folliat who led the way into the house and Poirot followed her. It was a gracious house, beautifully proportioned. Mrs Folliat went through a door on the left into a small daintily furnished sitting-room and on into the big drawing-room beyond, which was full of people who all seemed, at the moment, to be talking at once.

'George,' said Mrs Folliat, 'this is M. Poirot who is so kind as to come and help us. Sir George Stubbs.'

Sir George, who had been talking in a loud voice, swung round. He was a big man with a rather florid red face and a slightly unexpected beard. It gave a rather disconcerting effect of an actor who had not quite made up his mind whether he was playing the part of a country squire, or of a 'rough diamond' from the Dominions. It certainly did not suggest the navy, in spite of Michael Weyman's remarks. His manner and voice were jovial, but his eyes were small and shrewd, of a particularly penetrating pale blue.

He greeted Poirot heartily.

'We're so glad that your friend Mrs Oliver managed to persuade you to come,' he said. 'Quite a brain-wave on her part. You'll be an enormous attraction.'

He looked round a little vaguely.

'Hattie?' He repeated the name in a slightly sharper tone. 'Hattie!'

Lady Stubbs was reclining in a big arm-chair a little distance from the others. She seemed to be paying no attention to what was going on round her. Instead she was smiling down at her hand which was stretched out on the arm of the chair. She was turning it from left to right, so that a big solitaire emerald on her third finger caught the light in its green depths.

She looked up now in a slightly startled childlike way and said, 'How do you do?'

Poirot bowed over her hand.

Sir George continued his introductions.

'Mrs Masterton.'

Mrs Masterton was a somewhat monumental woman who reminded Poirot faintly of a bloodhound. She had a full underhung jaw and large, mournful, slightly blood-shot eyes.

She bowed and resumed her discourse in a deep voice which again made Poirot think of a bloodhound's baying note.

'This silly dispute about the tea tent has got to be settled, Jim,' she said forcefully. 'They've got to see sense about it. We can't have the whole show a fiasco because of these idiotic women's local feuds.'

'Oh, quite,' said the man addressed.

'Captain Warburton,' said Sir George.

Captain Warburton, who wore a check sports coat and had a vaguely horsy appearance, showed a lot of white teeth in a somewhat wolfish smile, then continued his conversation.

'Don't you worry, I'll settle it,' he said. 'I'll go and talk to them like a Dutch uncle. What about the fortune-telling tent? In the space by the magnolia? Or at the far end of the lawn by the rhododendrons?'

Sir George continued his introductions.

'Mr and Mrs Legge.'

A tall young man with his face peeling badly from sunburn grinned agreeably. His wife, an attractive freckled redhead, nodded in a friendly fashion, then plunged into controversy with Mrs Masterton, her agreeable high treble making a kind of duet with Mrs Masterton's deep bay.

'—*not* by the magnolia—a bottle-neck—'

'—one wants to disperse things—but if there's a queue—'

'—much cooler. I mean, with the sun full on the house—'

'—and the coconut shy can't be too near the house—the boys are so wild when they throw—'

'And this,' said Sir George, 'is Miss Brewis—who runs us all.'

Miss Brewis was seated behind the large silver tea tray.

She was a spare efficient-looking woman of forty-odd, with a brisk pleasant manner.

'How do you do, M. Poirot,' she said. 'I do hope you didn't have too crowded a journey? The trains are sometimes too terrible this time of year. Let me give you some tea. Milk? Sugar?'

'Very little milk, mademoiselle, and four lumps of sugar.' He added, as Miss Brewis dealt with his request, 'I see that you are all in a great state of activity.'

'Yes, indeed. There are always so many last-minute things to see to. And people let one down in the most extraordinary way nowadays. Over marquees, and tents and chairs and catering equipment. One has to keep *on* at them. I was on the telephone half the morning.'

'What about these pegs, Amanda?' said Sir George. 'And the extra putters for the clock golf?'

'That's all arranged, Sir George. Mr Benson at the golf club was most kind.'

She handed Poirot his cup.

'A sandwich, M. Poirot? Those are tomato and these are *paté*. But perhaps,' said Miss Brewis, thinking of the four lumps of sugar, 'you would rather have a cream cake?'

Poirot would rather have a cream cake, and helped himself to a particularly sweet and squelchy one.

Then, balancing it carefully on his saucer, he went and sat down by his hostess. She was still letting the light play over the jewel on her hand, and she looked up at him with a pleased child's smile.

'Look,' she said. 'It's pretty, isn't it?'

He had been studying her carefully. She was wearing a big coolie-style hat of vivid magenta straw. Beneath it her face showed its pinky reflection on the dead-white surface of her skin. She was heavily made up in an exotic un-English style. Dead-white matt skin; vivid cyclamen lips, mascara applied lavishly to the eyes. Her hair showed beneath the hat, black and smooth, fitting like a velvet cap. There was a languorous un-English beauty about the face. She was a creature of the tropical sun, caught, as it were, by chance in an English drawing-room. But it was the eyes that startled Poirot. They had a childlike, almost vacant, stare.

She had asked her question in a confidential childish way, and it was as though to a child that Poirot answered.

'It is a very lovely ring,' he said.

She looked pleased.

'George gave it to me yesterday,' she said, dropping her voice as though she were sharing a secret with him. 'He gives me lots of things. He's very kind.'

Poirot looked down at the ring again and the hand outstretched on the side of the chair. The nails were very long and varnished a deep puce.

Into his mind a quotation came: 'They toil not, neither do they spin...'

He certainly couldn't imagine Lady Stubbs toiling or spinning. And yet he would hardly have described her as a lily of the field. She was a far more artificial product.

'This is a beautiful room you have here, Madame,' he said, looking round appreciatively.

'I suppose it is,' said Lady Stubbs vaguely.

Her attention was still on her ring; her head on one side, she watched the green fire in its depths as her hand moved.

She said in a confidential whisper, 'D'you see? It's winking at me.'

She burst out laughing and Poirot had a sense of sudden shock. It was a loud uncontrolled laugh.

From across the room Sir George said: 'Hattie.'

His voice was quite kind but held a faint admonition. Lady Stubbs stopped laughing.

Poirot said in a conventional manner:

'Devonshire is a very lovely county. Do you not think so?'

'It's nice in the daytime,' said Lady Stubbs. 'When it doesn't rain,' she added mournfully. 'But there aren't any nightclubs.'

'Ah, I see. You like nightclubs?'

'Oh, *yes*,' said Lady Stubbs fervently.

'And why do you like nightclubs so much?'

'There is music and you dance. And I wear my nicest clothes and bracelets and rings. And all the other women have nice clothes and jewels, but not as nice as mine.'

She smiled with enormous satisfaction. Poirot felt a slight pang of pity.

'And all that amuses you very much?'

'Yes. I like the casino, too. Why are there not any casinos in England?'

'I have often wondered,' said Poirot, with a sigh. 'I do not think it would accord with the English character.'

She looked at him uncomprehendingly. Then she bent slightly towards him.

'I won sixty thousand francs at Monte Carlo once. I put it on number twenty-seven and it came up.'

'That must have been very exciting, Madame.'

'Oh, it *was*. George gives me money to play with—but usually I lose it.'

She looked disconsolate.

'That is sad.'

'Oh, it does not really matter. George is very rich. It is nice to be rich, don't you think so?'

'Very nice,' said Poirot gently.

'Perhaps, if I was not rich, I should look like Amanda.' Her gaze went to Miss Brewis at the tea table and studied her dispassionately. 'She is very ugly, don't you think?'

Miss Brewis looked up at that moment and across to where they were sitting. Lady Stubbs had not spoken loudly, but Poirot wondered whether Amanda Brewis had heard.

As he withdrew his gaze, his eyes met those of Captain Warburton. The Captain's glance was ironic and amused.

Poirot endeavoured to change the subject.

'Have you been very busy preparing for the fête?' he asked.

Hattie Stubbs shook her head.

'Oh, no, I think it is all very boring—very stupid. There are servants and gardeners. Why should not they make the preparations?'

'Oh, my dear.' It was Mrs Folliat who spoke. She had come to sit on the sofa nearby. 'Those are the ideas you were brought up with on your island estates. But life isn't like that in England these days. I wish it were.' She sighed. 'Nowadays one has to do nearly everything oneself.'

Lady Stubbs shrugged her shoulders.

'I think it is stupid. What is the good of being rich if one has to do everything oneself?'

'Some people find it fun,' said Mrs Folliat, smiling at her. 'I do really. Not all things, but some. I like gardening myself and I like preparing for a festivity like this one tomorrow.'

'It will be like a party?' asked Lady Stubbs hopefully.

'Just like a party—with lots and lots of people.'

'Will it be like Ascot? With big hats and everyone very chic?'

'Well, not quite like Ascot,' said Mrs Folliat. She added gently, 'But you must try and enjoy country things, Hattie. You should have helped us this morning, instead of staying in bed and not getting up until teatime.'

'I had a headache,' said Hattie sulkily. Then her mood changed and she smiled affectionately at Mrs Folliat.

'But I will be good tomorrow. I will do everything you tell me.'

'That's very sweet of you, dear.'

'I've got a new dress to wear. It came this morning. Come upstairs with me and look at it.'

Mrs Folliat hesitated. Lady Stubbs rose to her feet and said insistently:

'You must come. Please. It is a lovely dress. Come *now*!'

'Oh, very well.' Mrs Folliat gave a half-laugh and rose.

As she went out of the room, her small figure following Hattie's tall one, Poirot saw her face and was quite startled at the weariness on it which had replaced her smiling composure. It was as though, relaxed and off her guard for a moment, she no longer bothered to keep up the social mask. And yet—it seemed more than that. Perhaps she was suffering from some disease about which, like many women, she never spoke. She was not a person, he thought, who would care to invite pity or sympathy.

Captain Warburton dropped down in the chair Hattie Stubbs had just vacated. He, too, looked at the door through which the two women had just passed, but it was not of the older woman that he spoke. Instead he drawled, with a slight grin:

'Beautiful creature, isn't she?' He observed with the tail of his eye Sir George's exit through a French window with Mrs Masterton and Mrs Oliver in tow. 'Bowled over old George Stubbs all right. Nothing's too good for her! Jewels, mink, all the rest of it. Whether he realizes she's a bit wanting in the top storey, I've never discovered. Probably thinks it doesn't matter. After all, these financial johnnies don't ask for intellectual companionship.'

'What nationality is she?' Poirot asked curiously.

'Looks South American, I always think. But I believe she comes from the West Indies. One of those islands with sugar and rum and all that. One of the old families there—a creole, I don't mean a half-caste. All very intermarried, I believe, on these islands. Accounts for the mental deficiency.'

Young Mrs Legge came over to join them.

'Look here, Jim,' she said, 'you've got to be on my side. That tent's got to be where we all decided—on the far side of the lawn backing on the rhododendrons. It's the only possible place.'

'Ma Masterton doesn't think so.'

'Well, you've got to talk her out of it.'

He gave her his foxy smile.

'Mrs Masterton's my boss.'

'Wilfred Masterton's your boss. He's the M.P.'

'I dare say, but she should be. She's the one who wears the pants—and don't I know it.'

Sir George re-entered the window.

'Oh, there you are, Sally,' he said. 'We need you. You wouldn't think everyone could get het up over who butters the buns and who raffles a cake, and why the garden produce stall is where the fancy woollens was promised it should be. Where's Amy Folliat? She can deal with these people—about the only person who can.'

'She went upstairs with Hattie.'

'Oh, did she—?'

Sir George looked round in a vaguely helpless manner and Miss Brewis jumped up from where she was writing tickets, and said, 'I'll fetch her for you, Sir George.'

'Thank you, Amanda.'

Miss Brewis went out of the room.

'Must get hold of some more wire fencing,' murmured Sir George.

'For the fête?'

'No, no. To put up where we adjoin Hoodown Park in the woods. The old stuff's rotted away, and that's where they get through.'

'Who get through?'

'Trespassers!' ejaculated Sir George.

31

Sally Legge said amusedly:

'You sound like Betsy Trotwood campaigning against donkeys.'

'Betsy Trotwood? Who's she?' asked Sir George simply.

'Dickens.'

'Oh, Dickens. I read the *Pickwick Papers* once. Not bad. Not bad at all—surprised me. But, seriously, trespassers are a menace since they've started this Youth Hostel tomfoolery. They come out at you from everywhere wearing the most incredible shirts—boy this morning had one all covered with crawling turtles and things—made me think I'd been hitting the bottle or something. Half of them can't speak English—just gibber at you...' He mimicked: '"Oh, plees—yes, haf you—tell me—iss way to ferry?" I say no, it isn't, roar at them, and send them back where they've come from, but half the time they just blink and stare and don't understand. And the girls giggle. All kinds of nationalities, Italian, Yugoslavian, Dutch, Finnish—Eskimos I shouldn't be surprised! Half of them communists, I shouldn't wonder,' he ended darkly.

'Come now, George, don't get started on communists,' said Mrs Legge. 'I'll come and help you deal with the rabid women.'

She led him out of the window and called over her shoulder: 'Come on, Jim. Come and be torn to pieces in a good cause.'

'All right, but I want to put M. Poirot in the picture about the Murder Hunt since he's going to present the prizes.'

'You can do that presently.'

'I will await you here,' said Poirot agreeably.

In the ensuing silence, Alec Legge stretched himself out in his chair and sighed.

'Women!' he said. 'Like a swarm of bees.'

He turned his head to look out of the window.

'And what's it all about? Some silly garden fête that doesn't matter to anyone.'

'But obviously,' Poirot pointed out, 'there are those to whom it does matter.'

'Why can't people have some *sense*? Why can't they *think*? Think of the mess the whole world has got itself into. Don't they realize that the inhabitants of the globe are busy committing suicide?'

Poirot judged rightly that he was not intended to reply to this question. He merely shook his head doubtfully.

'Unless we can do something before it's too late...' Alec Legge broke off. An angry look swept over his face. 'Oh, yes,' he said, 'I know what you're thinking. That I'm nervy, neurotic—all the rest of it. Like those damned doctors. Advising rest and change and sea air. All right, Sally and I came down here and took the Mill Cottage for three months, and I've followed their prescription. I've fished and bathed and taken long walks and sunbathed—'

'I noticed that you had sunbathed, yes,' said Poirot politely.

'Oh, this?' Alec's hand went to his sore face. 'That's the result of a fine English summer for once in a way. But what's the *good* of it all? You can't get away from facing truth just by running away from it.'

'No, it is never any good running away.'

'And being in a rural atmosphere like this just makes you realize things more keenly—that and the incredible apathy of the people of this country. Even Sally, who's intelligent enough, is just the same. Why bother? That's what she says. It makes me mad! Why bother?'

'As a matter of interest, why do you?'

'Good God, you too?'

'No, it is not advice. It is just that I would like to know your answer.'

'Don't you see, somebody's got to do something.'

'And that somebody is you?'

'No, no, not me personally. One can't be *personal* in times like these.'

'I do not see why not. Even in "these times" as you call it, one is still a person.'

'But one shouldn't be! In times of stress, when it's a matter of life or death, one can't think of one's own insignificant ills or preoccupations.'

'I assure you, you are quite wrong. In the late war, during a severe air-raid, I was much less preoccupied by the thought of death than of the pain from a corn on my little toe. It surprised me at the time that it should be so. "Think," I said to myself, "at any moment now, death may come." But I was still conscious of my corn—indeed, I felt injured that I should have that to suffer as well as the fear of death. It was *because* I might die that every small personal matter in my life acquired increased importance. I have seen a woman knocked down in a street accident, with a broken leg, and she has burst out crying because she sees that there is a ladder in her stocking.'

'Which just shows you what fools women are!'

'It shows you what *people* are. It is, perhaps, that absorption in one's personal life that has led the human race to survive.'

Alec Legge gave a scornful laugh.

'Sometimes,' he said, 'I think it's a pity they ever did.'

'It is, you know,' Poirot persisted, 'a form of humility. And humility is valuable. There was a slogan that was written up in your underground railways here, I remember, during the war. "It all depends on *you*." It was composed, I think, by some eminent divine—but in my opinion it was a dangerous and undesirable doctrine. For it is not *true*. Everything does *not* depend on, say, Mrs Blank of Little-Blank-in-the-Marsh. And if she is led to think it does, it will not be good for her character. While she thinks of the part she can play in world affairs, the baby pulls over the kettle.'

'You are rather old-fashioned in your views, I think. Let's hear what your slogan would be.'

'I do not need to formulate one of my own. There is an older one in this country which contents me very well.'

'What is that?'

'"Put your trust in God, and keep your powder dry."'

'Well, well...' Alec Legge seemed amused. 'Most unexpected coming from you. Do you know what I should like to see done in this country?'

'Something, no doubt, forceful and unpleasant,' said Poirot, smiling.

Alec Legge remained serious.

'I should like to see every feeble-minded person put out—right out! Don't let them breed. If, for one generation, only the intelligent were allowed to breed, think what the result would be.'

'A very large increase of patients in the psychiatric wards, perhaps,' said Poirot dryly. 'One needs roots as well as flowers on a plant, Mr Legge. However large and beautiful the flowers, if the earthy roots are destroyed there will be no more flowers.' He added in a conversational tone: 'Would you consider Lady Stubbs a candidate for the lethal chamber?'

'Yes, indeed. What's the good of a woman like that? What contribution has she ever made to society? Has she ever had an idea in her head that wasn't of clothes or furs or jewels? As I say, what good is she?'

'You and I,' said Poirot blandly, 'are certainly much more intelligent than Lady Stubbs. But'—he shook his head sadly—'it is true, I fear, that we are not nearly so ornamental.'

'Ornamental...' Alec was beginning with a fierce snort, but he was interrupted by the re-entry of Mrs Oliver and Captain Warburton through the window.

CHAPTER 4

'You must come and see the clues and things for the Murder Hunt, M. Poirot,' said Mrs Oliver breathlessly.

Poirot rose and followed them obediently.

The three of them went across the hall and into a small room furnished plainly as a business office.

'Lethal weapons to your left,' observed Captain Warburton, waving his hand towards a small baize-covered card table. On it were laid out a small pistol, a piece of lead piping with a rusty sinister stain on it, a blue bottle labelled Poison, a length of clothes line and a hypodermic syringe.

'Those are the Weapons,' explained Mrs Oliver, 'and these are the Suspects.'

She handed him a printed card which he read with interest.

Agatha Christie

Suspects

Estelle Glynne	—	a beautiful and mysterious young woman, the guest of
Colonel Blunt	—	the local Squire, whose daughter
Joan	—	is married to
Peter Gaye	—	a young Atom Scientist.
Miss Willing	—	a housekeeper.
Quiett	—	a butler.
Maya Stavisky	—	a girl hiker.
Esteban Loyola	—	an uninvited guest.

Poirot blinked and looked towards Mrs Oliver in mute incomprehension.

'A magnificent Cast of Characters,' he said politely. 'But permit me to ask, Madame, what does the Competitor do?'

'Turn the card over,' said Captain Warburton.

Poirot did so.

On the other side was printed:

Name and address ....

Solution:

Name of Murderer: ....
Weapon: ....
Motive: ....
Time and Place: ....
Reasons for arriving at your conclusions: ....
....

'Everyone who enters gets one of these,' explained Captain Warburton rapidly. 'Also a notebook and pencil for copying clues. There will be six clues. You go on from one to the other like a Treasure Hunt, and the weapons are concealed in suspicious places. Here's the first clue. A snapshot. Everyone starts with one of these.'

Poirot took the small print from him and studied it with a frown. Then he turned it upside down. He still looked puzzled. Warburton laughed.

'Ingenious bit of trick photography, isn't it?' he said complacently. 'Quite simple once you know what it is.'

Poirot, who did not know what it was, felt a mounting annoyance.

'Some kind of barred window?' he suggested.

'Looks a bit like it, I admit. No, it's a section of a tennis net.'

'Ah.' Poirot looked again at the snapshot. 'Yes, it is as you say—quite obvious when you have been told what it is!'

'So much depends on how you look at a thing,' laughed Warburton.

'That is a very profound truth.'

'The second clue will be found in a box under the centre of the tennis net. In the box are this empty poison bottle—here, and a loose cork.'

'Only, you see,' said Mrs Oliver rapidly, 'it's a screw-topped bottle, so the *cork* is really the clue.'

'I know, Madame, that you are always full of ingenuity, but I do not quite see—'

Mrs Oliver interrupted him.

'Oh, but of course,' she said, 'there's a story. Like in a magazine serial—a synopsis.' She turned to Captain Warburton. 'Have you got the leaflets?'

'They've not come from the printers yet.'

'But they *promised*!'

'I know. I know. Everyone always promises. They'll be ready this evening at six. I'm going in to fetch them in the car.'

'Oh, good.'

Mrs Oliver gave a deep sigh and turned to Poirot.

'Well, I'll have to tell it you, then. Only I'm not very good at telling things. I mean if I write things, I get them perfectly clear, but if I talk, it always sounds the most frightful muddle; and that's why I never discuss my plots with anyone. I've learnt not to, because if I do, they just look at me blankly and say "—er—yes, but—I don't see what happened—and surely that can't possibly make a book." So damping. And *not* true, because when I write it, it does!'

Mrs Oliver paused for breath, and then went on:

'Well, it's like this. There's Peter Gaye who's a young Atom Scientist and he's suspected of being in the pay of the Communists, and he's married to this girl, Joan Blunt, and his first wife's dead, but she isn't, and she turns up because she's a secret agent, or perhaps not, I mean she may really *be* a hiker—and the wife's having an affair, and this man Loyola turns up either to meet Maya, or to spy upon her, and there's a blackmailing letter which might be from the housekeeper, or again it might be the butler, and the revolver's missing, and as you don't know who the

40

blackmailing letter's to, and the hypodermic syringe fell out at dinner, and after that it disappeared...'

Mrs Oliver came to a full stop, estimating correctly Poirot's reaction.

'I know,' she said sympathetically. 'It sounds just a muddle, but it isn't really—not in my head—and when you see the synopsis leaflet, you'll find it's quite clear.

'And, anyway,' she ended, 'the story doesn't really matter, does it? I mean, not to *you*. All you've got to do is to present the prizes—very nice prizes, the first's a silver cigarette case shaped like a revolver—and say how remarkably clever the solver has been.'

Poirot thought to himself that the solver would indeed have been clever. In fact, he doubted very much that there would be a solver. The whole plot and action of the Murder Hunt seemed to him to be wrapped in impenetrable fog.

'Well,' said Captain Warburton cheerfully, glancing at his wrist-watch, 'I'd better be off to the printers and collect.'

Mrs Oliver groaned.

'If they're not done—'

'Oh, they're done all right. I telephoned. So long.'

He left the room.

Mrs Oliver immediately clutched Poirot by the arm and demanded in a hoarse whisper:

'Well?'

'Well—what?'

'Have you found out anything? Or spotted anybody?'

Poirot replied with mild reproof in his tones:

'Everybody and everything seems to me completely normal.'

'Normal?'

'Well, perhaps that is not quite the right word. Lady Stubbs, as you say, is definitely subnormal, and Mr Legge would appear to be rather abnormal.'

'Oh, he's all right,' said Mrs Oliver impatiently. 'He's had a nervous breakdown.'

Poirot did not question the somewhat doubtful wording of this sentence but accepted it at its face value.

'Everybody appears to be in the expected state of nervous agitation, high excitement, general fatigue, and strong irritation, which are characteristic of preparations for this form of entertainment. If you could only indicate—'

'Sh!' Mrs Oliver grasped his arm again. 'Someone's coming.'

It was just like a bad melodrama, Poirot felt, his own irritation mounting.

The pleasant mild face of Miss Brewis appeared round the door.

'Oh, there you are, M. Poirot. I've been looking for you to show you your room.'

She led him up the staircase and along a passage to a big airy room looking out over the river.

'There is a bathroom just opposite. Sir George talks of adding more bathrooms, but to do so would sadly impair the proportions of the rooms. I hope you'll find everything quite comfortable.'

'Yes, indeed.' Poirot swept an appreciative eye over the small bookstand, the reading-lamp and the box labelled 'Biscuits' by the bedside. 'You seem, in this house, to have everything organized to perfection. Am I to congratulate you, or my charming hostess?'

'Lady Stubbs' time is fully taken up in being charming,' said Miss Brewis, a slightly acid note in her voice.

'A very decorative young woman,' mused Poirot.

'As you say.'

'But in other respects is she not, perhaps…' He broke off. '*Pardon*. I am indiscreet. I comment on something I ought not, perhaps, to mention.'

Miss Brewis gave him a steady look. She said dryly:

'Lady Stubbs knows perfectly well exactly what she is doing. Besides being, as you said, a very decorative young woman, she is also a very shrewd one.'

She had turned away and left the room before Poirot's eyebrows had fully risen in surprise. So that was what the efficient Miss Brewis thought, was it? Or had she merely said so for some reason of her own? And why had she made such a statement to him—to a newcomer? Because he *was* a newcomer, perhaps? And also because he was a foreigner. As Hercule Poirot had discovered by experience, there were many English people who considered that what one said to foreigners didn't count!

He frowned perplexedly, staring absentmindedly at the door out of which Miss Brewis had gone. Then he strolled over to the window and stood looking out. As he did so, he saw Lady Stubbs come out of the house with Mrs Folliat and they stood for a moment or two talking by the big magnolia tree. Then Mrs Folliat nodded a goodbye, picked up her gardening basket and gloves and trotted off down the drive. Lady Stubbs stood watching her for a moment, then absentmindedly pulled off a magnolia flower, smelt it and began slowly to walk down the path that led through the trees to the river. She looked just once over her shoulder before she disappeared from sight. From behind the magnolia tree Michael Weyman came quietly into view, paused a moment irresolutely and then followed the tall slim figure down into the trees.

A good-looking and dynamic young man, Poirot thought. With a more attractive personality, no doubt, than that of Sir George Stubbs...

But if so, what of it? Such patterns formed themselves eternally through life. Rich middle-aged unattractive husband, young and beautiful wife with or without sufficient mental development, attractive and susceptible young man. What was there in that to make Mrs Oliver utter a peremptory summons through the telephone? Mrs Oliver, no doubt, had a vivid imagination, but...

'But after all,' murmured Hercule Poirot to himself, 'I am not a consultant in adultery—or in incipient adultery.'

Could there really be anything in this extraordinary notion of Mrs Oliver's that something was wrong? Mrs Oliver was a singularly muddle-headed woman, and how she managed somehow or other to turn out coherent detective stories was beyond him, and yet, for all her muddle-headedness she often surprised him by her sudden perception of truth.

'The time is short—short,' he murmured to himself. '*Is* there something wrong here, as Mrs Oliver believes? I am inclined to think there is. But what? Who is there who could enlighten me? I need to know more, much more, about the people in this house. Who is there who could inform me?'

After a moment's reflection he seized his hat (Poirot never risked going out in the evening air with uncovered head), and hurried out of his room and down the stairs. He heard afar the dictatorial baying of Mrs Masterton's deep voice. Nearer at hand, Sir George's voice rose with an amorous intonation.

'Damned becoming that yashmak thing. Wish I had you in my harem, Sally. I shall come and have my fortune told a good deal tomorrow. What'll you tell me, eh?'

There was a slight scuffle and Sally Legge's voice said breathlessly:

'George, you mustn't.'

Poirot raised his eyebrows, and slipped out of a conveniently adjacent side door. He set off at top speed down a back drive which his sense of locality enabled him to predict would at some point join the front drive.

His manoeuvre was successful and enabled him—panting very slightly—to come up beside Mrs Folliat and relieve her in a gallant manner of her gardening basket.

'You permit, Madame?'

'Oh, thank you, M. Poirot, that's very kind of you. But it's not heavy.'

'Allow me to carry it for you to your home. You live near here?'

'I actually live in the lodge by the front gate. Sir George very kindly rents it to me.'

The lodge by the front gate of her former home... How did she really feel about *that*, Poirot wondered. Her composure was so absolute that he had no clue to her feelings. He changed the subject by observing:

'Lady Stubbs is much younger than her husband, is she not?'

'Twenty-three years younger.'

'Physically she is very attractive.'

Mrs Folliat said quietly:

'Hattie is a dear good child.'

It was not an answer he had expected. Mrs Folliat went on:

'I know her very well, you see. For a short time she was under my care.'

'I did not know that.'

'How should you? It is in a way a sad story. Her people had estates, sugar estates, in the West Indies. As a result of an earthquake, the house there was burned down and her parents and brothers and sisters all lost their lives. Hattie herself was at a convent in Paris and was thus suddenly left without any near relatives. It was considered advisable by the executors that Hattie should be chaperoned and introduced into society after she had spent a certain time abroad. I accepted the charge of her.' Mrs Folliat added with a dry smile: 'I can smarten myself up on occasions and, naturally, I had the necessary connections—in fact, the late Governor had been a close friend of ours.'

'Naturally, Madame, I understand all that.'

'It suited me very well—I was going through a difficult

time. My husband had died just before the outbreak of war. My elder son who was in the navy went down with his ship, my younger son, who had been out in Kenya, came back, joined the commandos and was killed in Italy. That meant three lots of death duties and this house had to be put up for sale. I myself was very badly off and I was glad of the distraction of having someone young to look after and travel about with. I became very fond of Hattie, all the more so, perhaps, because I soon realized that she was—shall we say—not fully capable of fending for herself? Understand me, M. Poirot, Hattie is *not* mentally deficient, but she *is* what country folk describe as "simple." She is easily imposed upon, over docile, completely open to suggestion. I think myself that it was a blessing that there was practically no money. If she had been an heiress her position might have been one of much greater difficulty. She was attractive to men and being of an affectionate nature was easily attracted and influenced—she had definitely to be looked after. When, after the final winding up of her parents' estate, it was discovered that the plantation was destroyed and there were more debts than assets, I could only be thankful that a man such as Sir George Stubbs had fallen in love with her and wanted to marry her.'

'Possibly—yes—it was a solution.'

'Sir George,' said Mrs Folliat, 'though he is a self-made man and—let us face it—a complete vulgarian, is kindly and fundamentally decent, besides being extremely wealthy. I don't think he would ever ask for *mental* companionship from a wife, which is just as well. Hattie is everything he wants. She displays clothes and jewels to perfection, is affectionate and willing, and is completely happy with him. I confess that I am very thankful that that is so, for I admit that I deliberately influenced her to accept him. If it had turned out badly'—her voice faltered a little—'it would have been my fault for urging her to marry a man so many years older than herself. You see, as I told you, Hattie is completely suggestible. Anyone she is with at the time can dominate her.'

'It seems to me,' said Poirot approvingly, 'that you made there a most prudent arrangement for her. I am not, like the English, romantic. To arrange a good marriage, one must take more than romance into consideration.'

He added:

'And as for this place here, Nasse House, it is a most beautiful spot. Quite, as the saying goes, out of this world.'

'Since Nasse had to be sold,' said Mrs Folliat, with a faint tremor in her voice, 'I am glad that Sir George bought it. It was requisitioned during the war by the Army and afterwards it might have been bought and made into a guest house or a school, the rooms cut up and partitioned, distorted out of their natural beauty. Our neighbours, the Fletchers, at Hoodown, had to sell their place and it is now a Youth Hostel. One is glad that young people should enjoy themselves—and fortunately Hoodown is late-Victorian, and of no great architectural merit, so that the alterations do not matter. I'm afraid some of the young people trespass on our grounds. It makes Sir George very angry. It's true that they have occasionally damaged the rare shrubs by hacking them about—they come through here trying to get a short cut to the ferry across the river.'

They were standing now by the front gate. The lodge, a small white one-storied building, lay a little back from the drive with a small railed garden round it.

Mrs Folliat took back her basket from Poirot with a word of thanks.

'I was always very fond of the lodge,' she said, looking at it affectionately. 'Merdle, our head gardener for thirty years, used to live there. I much prefer it to the top cottage, though that has been enlarged and modernized by Sir George. It had to be; we've got quite a young man now as head gardener, with a young wife—and these young women must have electric irons and modern cookers and television, and all that. One must go with the times…' She sighed. 'There is hardly a person left now on the estate from the old days—all new faces.'

'I am glad, Madame,' said Poirot, 'that you at least have found a haven.'

'You know those lines of Spenser's? "*Sleep after toyle, port after stormie seas, ease after war, death after life, doth greatly please…*"'

She paused and said without any change of tone: 'It's a very wicked world, M. Poirot. And there are very wicked people in the world. You probably know that as well as I do. I don't say so before the younger people, it might discourage them, but it's true… Yes, it's a very wicked world…'

She gave him a little nod, then turned and went into the lodge. Poirot stood still, staring at the shut door.

CHAPTER 5

In a mood of exploration Poirot went through the front gates and down the steeply twisting road that presently emerged on a small quay. A large bell with a chain had a notice upon it: 'Ring for the Ferry.' There were various boats moored by the side of the quay. A very old man with rheumy eyes, who had been leaning against a bollard, came shuffling towards Poirot.

'Du ee want the ferry, sir?'

'I thank you, no. I have just come down from Nasse House for a little walk.'

'Ah, 'tis up at Nasse yu are? Worked there as a boy, I did, and my son, he were head gardener there. But I did use to look after the boats. Old Squire Folliat, he was fair mazed about boats. Sail in all weathers, he would. The Major, now, his son, he didn't care for sailing. Horses, that's all he cared about. And a pretty packet went on 'em. That and the bottle—had a hard time with him, his wife did. Yu've seen her, maybe—lives at the Lodge now, she du.'

'Yes, I have just left her there now.'

'Her be a Folliat, tu, second cousin from over Tiverton way. A great one for the garden, she is, all them there flowering shrubs she had put in. Even when it was took over during the war, and the two young gentlemen was gone to the war, she still looked after they shrubs and kept 'em from being over-run.'

'It was hard on her, both her sons being killed.'

'Ah, she've had a hard life, she have, what with this and that. Trouble with her husband, and trouble with the young gentlemen, tu. Not Mr Henry. He was as nice a young gentleman as yu could wish, took after his grandfather, fond of sailing and went into the Navy as a matter of course, but Mr James, he caused her a lot of trouble. Debts and women it were, and then, tu, he were real wild in his temper. Born one of they as can't go straight. But the war suited him, as yu might say—give him his chance. Ah! There's many who can't go straight in peace who dies bravely in war.'

'So now,' said Poirot, 'there are no more Folliats at Nasse.'

The old man's flow of talk died abruptly.

'Just as yu say, sir.'

Poirot looked curiously at the old man.

'Instead you have Sir George Stubbs. What is thought locally of him?'

'Us understands,' said the old man, 'that he be powerful rich.'

His tone sounded dry and almost amused.

'And his wife?'

Agatha Christie

'Ah, she's a fine lady from London, she is. No use for gardens, not her. They du say, tu, as her du be wanting up here.'

He tapped his temple significantly.

'Not as her isn't always very nice spoken and friendly. Just over a year they've been here. Bought the place and had it all done up like new. I remember as though 'twere yesterday them arriving. Arrived in the evening, they did, day after the worst gale as I ever remember. Trees down right and left—one down across the drive and us had to get it sawn away in a hurry to get the drive clear for the car. And the big oak up along, that come down and brought a lot of others down with it, made a rare mess, it did.'

'Ah, yes, where the Folly stands now?'

The old man turned aside and spat disgustedly.

'Folly 'tis called and Folly 'tis—new-fangled nonsense. Never was no Folly in the old Folliats' time. Her ladyship's idea that Folly was. Put up not three weeks after they first come, and I've no doubt she talked Sir George into it. Rare silly it looks stuck up there among the trees, like a heathen temple. A nice summer-house now, made rustic like with stained glass. I'd have nothing against *that*.'

Poirot smiled faintly.

'The London ladies,' he said, 'they must have their fancies. It is sad that the day of the Folliats is over.'

'Don't ee never believe that, sir.' The old man gave a wheezy chuckle. 'Always be Folliats at Nasse.'

'But the house belongs to Sir George Stubbs.'

'That's as may be—but there's still a Folliat here. Ah! Rare and cunning the Folliats are!'

'What do you mean?'

The old man gave him a sly sideways glance.

'Mrs Folliat be living up tu Lodge, bain't she?' he demanded.

'Yes,' said Poirot slowly. 'Mrs Folliat is living at the Lodge and the world is very wicked, and all the people in it are very wicked.'

The old man stared at him.

'Ah,' he said. 'Yu've got something there, maybe.'

He shuffled away again.

'But what have I got?' Poirot asked himself with irritation as he slowly walked up the hill back to the house.

II

Hercule Poirot made a meticulous toilet, applying a scented pomade to his moustaches and twirling them to a ferocious couple of points. He stood back from the mirror and was satisfied with what he saw.

The sound of a gong resounded through the house, and he descended the stairs.

The butler, having finished a most artistic performance, crescendo, forte, diminuendo, rallentando, was just replacing the gong stick on its hook. His dark melancholy face showed pleasure.

Poirot thought to himself: '*A blackmailing letter from*

the housekeeper—or it may be the butler...' This butler looked as though blackmailing letters would be well within his scope. Poirot wondered if Mrs Oliver took her characters from life.

Miss Brewis crossed the hall in an unbecoming flowered chiffon dress and he caught up with her, asking as he did so:

'You have a housekeeper here?'

'Oh, no, M. Poirot. I'm afraid one doesn't run to niceties of that kind nowadays, except in a really large establishment, of course. Oh, no, I'm the housekeeper—more housekeeper than secretary, sometimes, in this house.'

She gave a short acid laugh.

'So you are the housekeeper?' Poirot considered her thoughtfully.

He could not see Miss Brewis writing a blackmailing letter. Now, an anonymous letter—that would be a different thing. He had known anonymous letters written by women not unlike Miss Brewis—solid, dependable women, totally unsuspected by those around them.

'What is your butler's name?' he asked.

'Henden.' Miss Brewis looked a little astonished.

Poirot recollected himself and explained quickly:

'I ask because I had a fancy I had seen him somewhere before.'

'Very likely,' said Miss Brewis. 'None of these people ever seem to stay in any place more than four months. They must soon have done the round of all the available situations in England. After all, it's not many people who can afford butlers and cooks nowadays.'

They came into the drawing-room, where Sir George, looking somehow rather unnatural in a dinner-jacket, was proffering sherry. Mrs Oliver, in iron-grey satin, was looking like an obsolete battleship, and Lady Stubbs' smooth black head was bent down as she studied the fashions in *Vogue*.

Alec and Sally Legge were dining and also Jim Warburton.

'We've a heavy evening ahead of us,' he warned them. 'No bridge tonight. All hands to the pumps. There are any amount of notices to print, and the big card for the Fortune Telling. What name shall we have? Madame Zuleika? Esmeralda? Or Romany Leigh, the Gipsy Queen?'

'The Eastern touch,' said Sally. 'Everyone in agricultural districts hates gipsies. Zuleika sounds all right. I brought my paint box over and I thought Michael could do us a curling snake to ornament the notice.'

'Cleopatra rather than Zuleika, then?'

Henden appeared at the door.

'Dinner is served, my lady.'

They went in. There were candles on the long table. The room was full of shadows.

Warburton and Alec Legge sat on either side of their hostess. Poirot was between Mrs Oliver and Miss Brewis. The latter was engaged in brisk general conversation about further details of preparation for tomorrow.

Mrs Oliver sat in brooding abstraction and hardly spoke.

When she did at last break her silence, it was with a somewhat contradictory explanation.

'Don't bother about me,' she said to Poirot. 'I'm just remembering if there's anything I've forgotten.'

55

Sir George laughed heartily.

'The fatal flaw, eh?' he remarked.

'That's just it,' said Mrs Oliver. 'There always is one. Sometimes one doesn't realize it until a book's actually in print. And then it's *agony*!' Her face reflected this emotion. She sighed. 'The curious thing is that most people never notice it. I say to myself, "But of course the cook would have been bound to notice that two cutlets hadn't been eaten." But nobody else thinks of it at all.'

'You fascinate me.' Michael Weyman leant across the table. 'The Mystery of the Second Cutlet. Please, please never explain. I shall wonder about it in my bath.'

Mrs Oliver gave him an abstracted smile and relapsed into her preoccupations.

Lady Stubbs was also silent. Now and again she yawned. Warburton, Alec Legge and Miss Brewis talked across her.

As they came out of the dining-room, Lady Stubbs stopped by the stairs.

'I'm going to bed,' she announced. 'I'm very sleepy.'

'Oh, Lady Stubbs,' exclaimed Miss Brewis, 'there's so much to be done. We've been counting on you to help us.'

'Yes, I know,' said Lady Stubbs. 'But I'm going to bed.'

She spoke with the satisfaction of a small child.

She turned her head as Sir George came out of the dining-room.

'I'm tired, George. I'm going to bed. You don't mind?'

He came up to her and patted her on the shoulder affectionately.

'You go and get your beauty sleep, Hattie. Be fresh for tomorrow.'

He kissed her lightly and she went up the stairs, waving her hand and calling out:

'Goodnight, all.'

Sir George smiled up at her. Miss Brewis drew in her breath sharply and turned brusquely away.

'Come along, everybody,' she said, with a forced cheerfulness that did not ring true. 'We've got to *work*.'

Presently everyone was set to their tasks. Since Miss Brewis could not be everywhere at once, there were soon some defaulters. Michael Weyman ornamented a placard with a ferociously magnificent serpent and the words, *Madame Zuleika will tell your Fortune*, and then vanished unobtrusively. Alec Legge did a few nondescript chores and then went out avowedly to measure for the hoop-la and did not reappear. The women, as women do, worked energetically and conscientiously. Hercule Poirot followed his hostess's example and went early to bed.

III

Poirot came down to breakfast on the following morning at nine-thirty. Breakfast was served in pre-war fashion. A row of hot dishes on an electric heater. Sir George was eating a full-sized Englishman's breakfast of scrambled eggs, bacon and kidneys. Mrs Oliver and Miss Brewis had a modified version of the same. Michael Weyman was eating a plateful of cold ham. Only Lady Stubbs was unheedful of the fleshpots and was nibbling thin toast and sipping black coffee. She was wearing a large pale-pink hat which looked odd at the breakfast table.

The post had just arrived. Miss Brewis had an enormous pile of letters in front of her which she was rapidly sorting into piles. Any of Sir George's marked 'Personal' she passed over to him. The others she opened herself and sorted into categories.

Lady Stubbs had three letters. She opened what were clearly a couple of bills and tossed them aside. Then she opened the third letter and said suddenly and clearly:

'Oh!'

The exclamation was so startled that all heads turned towards her.

'It's from Etienne,' she said. 'My cousin Etienne. He's coming here in a yacht.'

'Let's see, Hattie.' Sir George held out his hand. She passed the letter down the table. He smoothed out the sheet and read.

'Who's this Etienne de Sousa? A cousin, you say?'

'I think so. A second cousin. I do not remember him very well—hardly at all. He was—'

'Yes, my dear?'

She shrugged her shoulders.

'It does not matter. It is all a long time ago. I was a little girl.'

'I suppose you wouldn't remember him very well. But we must make him welcome, of course,' said Sir George heartily. 'Pity in a way it's the fête today, but we'll ask him to dinner. Perhaps we could put him up for a night or two—show him something of the country?'

Sir George was being the hearty country squire.

Lady Stubbs said nothing. She stared down into her coffee-cup.

Conversation on the inevitable subject of the fête became general. Only Poirot remained detached, watching the slim exotic figure at the head of the table. He wondered just what was going on in her mind. At that very moment her eyes came up and cast a swift glance along the table to where he sat. It was a look so shrewd and appraising that he was startled. As their eyes met, the shrewd expression vanished—emptiness returned. But that other look had been there, cold, calculating, watchful...

Or had he imagined it? In any case, wasn't it true that people who were slightly mentally deficient very often had a kind of sly native cunning that sometimes surprised even the people who knew them best?

He thought to himself that Lady Stubbs was certainly an enigma. People seemed to hold diametrically opposite ideas concerning her. Miss Brewis had intimated that Lady Stubbs knew very well what she was doing. Yet Mrs Oliver definitely thought her halfwitted, and Mrs Folliat who had known her long and intimately had spoken of her as someone not quite normal, who needed care and watchfulness.

Miss Brewis was probably prejudiced. She disliked Lady Stubbs for her indolence and her aloofness. Poirot wondered if Miss Brewis had been Sir George's secretary prior to his marriage. If so, she might easily resent the coming of the new regime.

Poirot himself would have agreed wholeheartedly with Mrs Folliat and Mrs Oliver—until this morning. And, after all, could he really rely on what had been only a fleeting impression?

Lady Stubbs got up abruptly from the table.

'I have a headache,' she said. 'I shall go and lie down in my room.'

Sir George sprang up anxiously.

'My dear girl. You're all right, aren't you?'

'It's just a headache.'

'You'll be fit enough for this afternoon, won't you?'

'Yes, I think so.'

'Take some aspirin, Lady Stubbs,' said Miss Brewis briskly. 'Have you got some or shall I bring it to you?'

'I've got some.'

She moved towards the door. As she went she dropped the handkerchief she had been squeezing between her fingers. Poirot, moving quietly forward, picked it up unobtrusively.

Sir George, about to follow his wife, was stopped by Miss Brewis.

'About the parking of cars this afternoon, Sir George. I'm just going to give Mitchell instructions. Do you think that the best plan would be, as you said—?'

Poirot, going out of the room, heard no more.

He caught up his hostess on the stairs.

'Madame, you dropped this.'

He proffered the handkerchief with a bow.

She took it unheedingly.

'Did I? Thank you.'

'I am most distressed, Madame, that you should be suffering. Particularly when your cousin is coming.'

She answered quickly, almost violently.

'I don't want to see Etienne. I don't like him. He's bad. He was always bad. I'm afraid of him. He does bad things.'

The door of the dining-room opened and Sir George came across the hall and up the stairs.

'Hattie, my poor darling. Let me come and tuck you up.'

They went up the stairs together, his arm round her tenderly, his face worried and absorbed.

Poirot looked up after them, then turned to encounter Miss Brewis moving fast, and clasping papers.

'Lady Stubbs' headache—' he began.

'No more headache than my foot,' said Miss Brewis crossly, and disappeared into her office, closing the door behind her.

Poirot sighed and went out through the front door on to the terrace. Mrs Masterton had just driven up in a small car and was directing the elevation of a tea marquee, baying out orders in rich full-blooded tones.

She turned to greet Poirot.

'Such a nuisance, these affairs,' she observed. 'And they will always put everything in the wrong place. No, Rogers! More to the left—*left*—not right! What do you think of the weather, M. Poirot? Looks doubtful to me. Rain, of course, would spoil everything. And we've had such a fine summer this year for a change. Where's Sir George? I want to talk to him about car parking.'

'His wife had a headache and has gone to lie down.'

'She'll be all right this afternoon,' said Mrs Masterton confidently. 'Likes functions, you know. She'll make a terrific toilet and be as pleased about it as a child. Just fetch me a bundle of those pegs over there, will you? I want to mark the places for the clock golf numbers.'

Poirot, thus pressed into service, was worked by Mrs Masterton relentlessly, as a useful apprentice. She condescended to talk to him in the intervals of hard labour.

'Got to do everything yourself, I find. Only way... By the way, you're a friend of the Eliots, I believe?'

Poirot, after his long sojourn in England, comprehended that this was an indication of social recognition. Mrs Masterton was in fact saying: 'Although a foreigner, I understand you are One of Us.' She continued to chat in an intimate manner.

'Nice to have Nasse lived in again. We were all so afraid it was going to be a hotel. You know what it is nowadays; one drives through the country and passes place after place with the board up "Guest House" or "Private Hotel" or "Hotel A.A. Fully Licensed." All the houses one stayed in as a girl—or where one went to dances. Very sad. Yes, I'm glad about Nasse and so is poor dear Amy Folliat, of course. She's had such a hard life—but never complains, I will say. Sir George has done wonders for Nasse—and *not* vulgarized it. Don't know whether that's the result of Amy Folliat's influence—or whether it's his own natural good taste. He *has* got quite good taste, you know. Very surprising in a man like that.'

'He is not, I understand, one of the landed gentry?' said Poirot cautiously.

'He isn't even really Sir George—was christened it, I understand. Took the idea from Lord George Sanger's Circus, I suspect. Very amusing really. Of course we never let on. Rich men must be allowed their little snobberies, don't you agree? The funny thing is that in spite of his origins George Stubbs would go down perfectly well anywhere. He's a throwback. Pure type of the eighteenth-century country squire. Good blood in him, I'd say. Father a gent and mother a barmaid, is my guess.'

Mrs Masterton interrupted herself to yell to a gardener.

'Not by that rhododendron. You must leave room for the skittles over to the right. *Right*—not left!'

She went on: 'Extraordinary how they can't tell their left from their right. The Brewis woman is efficient. Doesn't like poor Hattie, though. Looks at her sometimes as though she'd like to murder her. So many of these good secretaries are in love with their boss. Now where do you think Jim Warburton can have got to? Silly the way he sticks to calling himself "Captain." Not a regular soldier and never within miles of a German. One has to put up, of course, with what one can get these days—and he's a hard worker—but I feel there's something rather fishy about him. Ah! Here are the Legges.'

Sally Legge, dressed in slacks and a yellow pullover, said brightly:

'We've come to help.'

'Lots to do,' boomed Mrs Masterton. 'Now, let me see…'

Poirot, profiting by her inattention, slipped away. As he came round the corner of the house on to the front terrace he became a spectator of a new drama.

Two young women, in shorts, with bright blouses, had come out from the wood and were standing uncertainly looking up at the house. In one of them he thought he recognized the Italian girl of yesterday's lift in the car. From the window of Lady Stubbs' bedroom Sir George leaned out and addressed them wrathfully.

'You're trespassing,' he shouted.

'Please?' said the young woman with the green headscarf.

'You can't come through here. Private.'

The other young woman, who had a royal blue headscarf, said brightly:

'Please? Nassecombe Quay…' She pronounced it carefully. 'It is this way? Please.'

'You're trespassing,' bellowed Sir George.

'Please?'

'*Trespassing!* No way through. You've got to go back. *BACK!* The way you came.'

They stared as he gesticulated. Then they consulted together in a flood of foreign speech. Finally, doubtfully, blue-scarf said:

'Back? To Hostel?'

'That's right. And you take the road—*road* round that way.'

They retreated unwillingly. Sir George mopped his brow and looked down at Poirot.

'Spend my time turning people off,' he said. 'Used to come through the top gate. I've padlocked that. Now they come through the woods, having got over the fence. Think they can get down to the shore and the quay easily this way. Well, they can, of course, much quicker. But there's no right of way—never has been. And they're practically all foreigners—don't understand what you say, and just jabber back at you in Dutch or something.'

'Of these, one is German and the other Italian, I think—I saw the Italian girl on her way from the station yesterday.'

'Every kind of language they talk... Yes, Hattie? What did you say?' He drew back into the room.

Poirot turned to find Mrs Oliver and a well-developed girl of fourteen dressed in Guide uniform close behind him.

'This is Marlene,' said Mrs Oliver.

Marlene giggled.

'I'm the horrible Corpse,' she said. 'But I'm not going to have any blood on me.' Her tone expressed disappointment.

'No?'

'No. Just strangled with a cord, that's all. I'd of *liked* to be stabbed—and have lashings of red paint.'

'Captain Warburton thought it might look too realistic,' said Mrs Oliver.

'In a murder I think you *ought* to have blood,' said Marlene sulkily. She looked at Poirot with hungry interest. 'Seen lots of murders, haven't you? So *she* says.'

'One or two,' said Poirot modestly.

He observed with alarm that Mrs Oliver was leaving them.

'Any sex maniacs?' asked Marlene with avidity.

'Certainly not.'

'I like sex maniacs,' said Marlene with relish. 'Reading about them, I mean.'

'You would probably not like meeting one.'

'Oh, I dunno. D'you know what? I believe we've got a sex maniac round here. My granddad saw a body in the woods once. He was scared and ran away, and when he come back it was gone. It was a woman's body. But of course he's batty, my granddad is, so no one listens to what he says.'

Poirot managed to escape and, regaining the house by a circuitous route, took refuge in his bedroom. He felt in need of repose.

CHAPTER 6

Lunch was an early and quickly snatched affair of a cold buffet. At two-thirty a minor film star was to open the fête. The weather, after looking ominously like rain, began to improve. By three o'clock the fête was in full swing. People were paying the admission charge of half a crown in large numbers, and cars were lining one side of the long drive. Students from the Youth Hostel arrived in batches conversing loudly in foreign tongues. True to Mrs Masterton's forecast, Lady Stubbs had emerged from her bedroom just before half-past two, dressed in a cyclamen dress with an enormous coolie-shaped hat of black straw. She wore large quantities of diamonds.

Miss Brewis murmured sardonically:

'Thinks it's the Royal Enclosure at Ascot, evidently!'

But Poirot complimented her gravely.

'It is a beautiful creation that you have on, Madame.'

'It is nice, isn't it,' said Hattie happily. 'I wore it for Ascot.'

The minor film star was arriving and Hattie moved forward to greet her.

Poirot retreated into the background. He wandered around disconsolately—everything seemed to be proceeding in the normal fashion of fêtes. There was a coconut shy, presided over by Sir George in his heartiest fashion, a skittle alley and a hoop-la. There were various 'stalls' displaying local produce of fruit, vegetables, jams and cakes—and others displaying 'fancy objects.' There were 'raffles' of cakes, of baskets of fruit; even, it seemed, of a pig; and a 'Lucky Dip' for children at twopence a go.

There was a good crowd of people by now and an Exhibition of Children's Dancing began. Poirot saw no sign of Mrs Oliver, but Lady Stubbs' cyclamen pink figure showed up amongst the crowd as she drifted rather vaguely about. The focus of attention, however, seemed to be Mrs Folliat. She was quite transformed in appearance—wearing a hydrangea-blue foulard frock and a smart grey hat, she appeared to preside over the proceedings, greeting new arrivals, and directing people to the various side shows.

Poirot lingered near her and listened to some of the conversations.

'Amy, my dear, how are you?'

'Oh, Pamela, how nice of you and Edward to come. Such a long way from Tiverton.'

'The weather's held for you. Remember the year before the war? Cloudburst came down about four o'clock. Ruined the whole show.'

'But it's been a wonderful summer this year. Dorothy! It's *ages* since I've seen you.'

'We felt we *had* to come and see Nasse in its glory. I see you've cut back the berberis on the bank.'

'Yes, it shows the hydrangeas better, don't you think?'

'How wonderful they are. What a blue! But, my dear, you've done wonders in the last year. Nasse is really beginning to look like itself again.'

Dorothy's husband boomed in a deep voice:

'Came over to see the commandant here during the war. Nearly broke my heart.'

Mrs Folliat turned to greet a humbler visitor.

'Mrs Knapper, I am pleased to see you. Is this Lucy? How she's grown!'

'She'll be leaving school next year. Pleased to see you looking so well, ma'am.'

'I'm very well, thank you. You must go and try your luck at hoop-la, Lucy. See you in the tea tent later, Mrs Knapper. I shall be helping with the teas.'

An elderly man, presumably Mr Knapper, said diffidently:

'Pleased to have you back at Nasse, ma'am. Seems like old times.'

Mrs Folliat's response was drowned as two women and a big beefy man rushed towards her.

'Amy, dear, such *ages*. This looks the *greatest* success! Do tell me what you've done about the rose garden. Muriel told me that you're restocking it with all the new floribundas.'

The beefy man chipped in.

'Where's Marylin Gale—?'

'Reggie's just dying to meet her. He saw her last picture.'

'That her in the big hat? My word, that's some get-up.'

'Don't be stupid, darling. That's Hattie Stubbs. You know, Amy, you really shouldn't let her go round *quite* so like a mannequin.'

'Amy?' Another friend claimed attention. 'This is Roger, Edward's boy. My dear, so nice to have you back at Nasse.'

Poirot moved slowly away and absent-mindedly invested a shilling on a ticket that might win him the pig.

He heard faintly still, the 'So good of you to come' refrain from behind him. He wondered whether Mrs Folliat real-ized how completely she had slipped into the role of hostess or whether it was entirely unconscious. She was, very defi-nitely this afternoon, Mrs Folliat of Nasse House.

He was standing by the tent labelled '*Madame Zuleika will tell your Fortune for 2s. 6d.*' Teas had just begun to be served and there was no longer a queue for the fortune telling. Poirot bowed his head, entered the tent and paid over his half-crown willingly for the privilege of sinking into a chair and resting his aching feet.

Madame Zuleika was wearing flowing black robes, a gold tinsel scarf wound round her head and a veil across the lower half of her face which slightly muffled her remarks. A gold bracelet hung with lucky charms tinkled as she took Poirot's hand and gave him a rapid reading, agreeably full of money to come, success with a dark beauty and a miracu-lous escape from an accident.

'It is very agreeable all that you tell me, Madame Legge. I only wish that it could come true.'

'Oh!' said Sally. 'So you know me, do you?'

'I had advance information—Mrs Oliver told me that

you were originally to be the "victim," but that you had been snatched from her for the Occult.'

'I wish I *was* being the "body,"' said Sally. 'Much more peaceful. All Jim Warburton's fault. Is it four o'clock yet? I want my tea. I'm off duty from four to half-past.'

'Ten minutes to go, still,' said Poirot, consulting his large old-fashioned watch. 'Shall I bring you a cup of tea here?'

'No, no. I want the break. This tent is stifling. Are there a lot of people waiting still?'

'No. I think they are lining up for tea.'

'Good.'

Poirot emerged from the tent and was immediately challenged by a determined woman and made to pay sixpence and guess the weight of a cake.

A hoop-la stall presided over by a fat motherly woman urged him to try his luck and, much to his discomfiture, he immediately won a large Kewpie doll. Walking sheepishly along with this he encountered Michael Weyman who was standing gloomily on the outskirts near the top of a path that led down to the quay.

'You seem to have been enjoying yourself, M. Poirot,' he said, with a sardonic grin.

Poirot contemplated his prize.

'It is truly horrible, is it not?' he said sadly.

A small child near him suddenly burst out crying. Poirot stooped swiftly and tucked the doll into the child's arm.

'*Voilà*, it is for you.'

The tears ceased abruptly.

'There—Violet—isn't the gentleman kind? Say, Ta, ever so—'

'Children's Fancy Dress,' called out Captain Warburton through a megaphone. 'The first class—three to five. Form up, please.'

Poirot moved towards the house and was cannoned into by a young man who was stepping backwards to take a better aim at a coconut. The young man scowled and Poirot apologized, mechanically, his eye held fascinated by the varied pattern of the young man's shirt. He recognized it as the 'turtle' shirt of Sir George's description. Every kind of turtle, tortoise and sea monster appeared to be writhing and crawling over it.

Poirot blinked and was accosted by the Dutch girl to whom he had given a lift the day before.

'So you have come to the fête,' he said. 'And your friend?'

'Oh, yes, she, too, comes here this afternoon. I have not seen her yet, but we shall leave together by the bus that goes from the gates at five-fifteen. We go to Torquay and there I change to another bus for Plymouth. It is convenient.'

This explained what had puzzled Poirot, the fact that the Dutch girl was perspiring under the weight of a rucksack.

He said: 'I saw your friend this morning.'

'Oh, yes, Elsa, a German girl, was with her and she told me they had tried to get through woods to the river and quay. And the gentleman who owns the house was very angry and made them go back.'

She added, turning her head to where Sir George was urging competitors on at the coconut shy:

'But now—this afternoon, he is very polite.'

Poirot considered explaining that there was a difference between young women who were trespassers and the same young women when they had paid two shillings and sixpence entrance fee and were legally entitled to sample the delights of Nasse House and its grounds. But Captain Warburton and his megaphone bore down upon him. The Captain was looking hot and bothered.

'Have you seen Lady Stubbs, Poirot? Anyone seen Lady Stubbs? She's supposed to be judging this Fancy Dress business and I can't find her anywhere.'

'I saw her, let me see—oh, about half an hour ago. But then I went to have my fortune told.'

'Curse the woman,' said Warburton angrily. 'Where can she have disappeared to? The children are waiting and we're behind schedule as it is.'

He looked round.

'Where's Amanda Brewis?'

Miss Brewis, also, was not in evidence.

'It really is too bad,' said Warburton. 'One's got to have *some* co-operation if one's trying to run a show. Where *can* Hattie be? Perhaps she's gone into the house.'

He strode off rapidly.

Poirot edged his way towards the roped-off space where teas were being served in a large marquee, but there was a long queue waiting and he decided against it.

He inspected the Fancy Goods stall where a determined old lady very nearly managed to sell him a plastic collar box, and finally made his way round the outskirts to a place where he could contemplate the activity from a safe distance.

He wondered where Mrs Oliver was.

Footsteps behind him made him turn his head. A young

man was coming up the path from the quay; a very dark young man, faultlessly attired in yachting costume. He paused as though disconcerted by the scene before him.

Then he spoke hesitatingly to Poirot.

'You will excuse me. Is this the house of Sir George Stubbs?'

'It is indeed.' Poirot paused and then hazarded a guess. 'Are you, perhaps, the cousin of Lady Stubbs?'

'I am Etienne de Sousa—'

'My name is Hercule Poirot.'

They bowed to each other. Poirot explained the circumstances of the fête. As he finished, Sir George came across the lawn towards them from the coconut shy.

'De Sousa? Delighted to see you. Hattie got your letter this morning. Where's your yacht?'

'It is moored at Helmmouth. I came up the river to the quay here in my launch.'

'We must find Hattie. She's somewhere about... You'll dine with us this evening, I hope?'

'You are most kind.'

'Can we put you up?'

'That also is most kind, but I will sleep on my yacht. It is easier so.'

'Are you staying here long?'

'Two or three days, perhaps. It depends.' De Sousa shrugged elegant shoulders.

'Hattie will be delighted, I'm sure,' said Sir George politely. 'Where *is* she? I saw her not long ago.'

He looked round in a perplexed manner.

'She ought to be judging the children's fancy dress. I

can't understand it. Excuse me a moment. I'll ask Miss Brewis.'

He hurried off. De Sousa looked after him. Poirot looked at De Sousa.

'It is some little time since you last saw your cousin?' he asked.

The other shrugged his shoulders.

'I have not seen her since she was fifteen years old. Soon after that she was sent abroad—to school at a convent in France. As a child she promised to have good looks.'

He looked inquiringly at Poirot.

'She is a beautiful woman,' said Poirot.

'And that is her husband? He seems what they call "a good fellow," but not perhaps very polished? Still, for Hattie it might be perhaps a little difficult to find a suitable husband.'

Poirot remained with a politely inquiring expression on his face. The other laughed.

'Oh, it is no secret. At fifteen Hattie was mentally undeveloped. Feeble minded, do you not call it? She is still the same?'

'It would seem so—yes,' said Poirot cautiously.

De Sousa shrugged his shoulders.

'Ah, well! Why should one ask it of women—that they should be intelligent? It is not necessary.'

Sir George was back, fuming. Miss Brewis was with him, speaking rather breathlessly.

'I've no idea where she is, Sir George. I saw her over by the fortune teller's tent last. But that was at least twenty minutes or half an hour ago. She's not in the house.'

'Is it not possible,' asked Poirot, 'that she has gone to observe the progress of Mrs Oliver's murder hunt?'

Sir George's brow cleared.

'That's probably it. Look here, I can't leave the shows here. I'm in charge. And Amanda's got her hands full. Could *you* possibly have a look round, Poirot? You know the course.'

But Poirot did not know the course. However, an inquiry of Miss Brewis gave him rough guidance. Miss Brewis took brisk charge of De Sousa and Poirot went off murmuring to himself, like an incantation: 'Tennis Court, Camellia Garden, The Folly, Upper Nursery Garden, Boathouse...'

As he passed the coconut shy he was amused to notice Sir George proffering wooden balls with a dazzling smile of welcome to the same young Italian woman whom he had driven off that morning and who was clearly puzzled at his change of attitude.

He went on his way to the tennis court. But there was no one there but an old gentleman of military aspect who was fast asleep on a garden seat with his hat pulled over his eyes. Poirot retraced his steps to the house and went on down to the camellia garden.

In the camellia garden Poirot found Mrs Oliver dressed in purple splendour, sitting on a garden seat in a brooding attitude, and looking rather like Mrs Siddons. She beckoned him to the seat beside her.

'This is only the second clue,' she hissed. 'I think I've made them too difficult. Nobody's come yet.'

At this moment a young man in shorts, with a prominent Adam's apple, entered the garden. With a cry of satisfaction he hurried to a tree in one corner and a further satisfied cry announced his discovery of the next clue. Passing them, he felt impelled to communicate his satisfaction.

'Lots of people don't know about cork trees,' he said confidentially. 'Clever photograph, the first clue, but I spotted what it was—section of a tennis net. There was a poison bottle, empty, and a cork. Most of 'em will go all out after the bottle clue—I guessed it was a red herring. Very delicate, cork trees, only hardy in this part of the world. I'm interested in rare shrubs and trees. *Now* where does one go, I wonder?'

He frowned over the entry in the notebook he carried.

'I've copied the next clue but it doesn't seem to make sense.' He eyed them suspiciously. 'You competing?'

'Oh, no,' said Mrs Oliver. 'We're just—looking on.'

'Righty-ho…" *When lovely woman stoops to folly*."… I've an idea I've heard that somewhere.'

'It is a well-known quotation,' said Poirot.

'A Folly can also be a building,' said Mrs Oliver helpfully. 'White—with pillars,' she added.

'*That's* an idea! Thanks a lot. They say Mrs Ariadne Oliver is down here herself somewhere about. I'd like to get her autograph. You haven't seen her about, have you?'

'No,' said Mrs Oliver firmly.

'I'd like to meet her. Good yarns she writes.' He lowered his voice. 'But they say she drinks like a fish.'

He hurried off and Mrs Oliver said indignantly:

'Really! That's most unfair when I only like lemonade!'

'And have you not just perpetrated the greatest unfairness in helping that young man towards the next clue?'

'Considering he's the only one who's got here so far, I thought he ought to be encouraged.'

'But you wouldn't give him your autograph.'

'That's different,' said Mrs Oliver. 'Sh! Here come some more.'

But these were not clue hunters. They were two women who having paid for admittance were determined to get their money's worth by seeing the grounds thoroughly.

They were hot and dissatisfied.

'You'd think they'd have *some* nice flower-beds,' said one to the other. 'Nothing but trees and more trees. It's not what I call a *garden.*'

Mrs Oliver nudged Poirot, and they slipped quietly away.

'Supposing,' said Mrs Oliver distractedly, 'that *nobody* ever finds my body?'

'Patience, Madame, and courage,' said Poirot. 'The afternoon is still young.'

'That's true,' said Mrs Oliver, brightening. 'And it's half-price admission after four-thirty, so probably lots of people will flock in. Let's go and see how that Marlene child is getting on. I don't really trust that girl, you know. No sense of responsibility. I wouldn't put it past her to sneak away quietly, instead of being a corpse, and go and have tea. You know what people are like about their teas.'

They proceeded amicably along the woodland path and Poirot commented on the geography of the property.

'I find it very confusing,' he said. 'So many paths, and one is never sure where they lead. And trees, trees everywhere.'

'You sound like that disgruntled woman we've just left.'

They passed the Folly and zig-zagged down the path to the river. The outlines of the boathouse showed beneath them.

Poirot remarked that it would be awkward if the murder searchers were to light upon the boathouse and find the body by accident.

'A sort of short cut? I thought of that. That's why the last clue is just a key. You can't unlock the door without it. It's a Yale. You can only open it from the inside.'

A short steep slope led down to the door of the boathouse which was build out over the river, with a little wharf and a storage place for boats underneath. Mrs Oliver took a key from a pocket concealed amongst her purple folds and unlocked the door.

'We've just come to cheer you up, Marlene,' she said brightly as she entered.

She felt slightly remorseful at her unjust suspicions of Marlene's loyalty, for Marlene, artistically arranged as 'the body,' was playing her part nobly, sprawled on the floor by the window.

Marlene made no response. She lay quite motionless. The wind blowing gently through the open window rustled a pile of 'comics' spread out on the table.

'It's all right,' said Mrs Oliver impatiently. 'It's only me and M. Poirot. Nobody's got any distance with the clues yet.'

Poirot was frowning. Very gently he pushed Mrs Oliver aside and went and bent over the girl on the floor. A suppressed exclamation came from his lips. He looked up at Mrs Oliver.

'So...' he said. 'That which you expected has happened.'

'You don't mean…' Mrs Oliver's eyes widened in horror. She grasped for one of the basket chairs and sat down. 'You can't mean… She isn't *dead*?'

Poirot nodded.

'Oh, yes,' he said. 'She is dead. Though not very long dead.'

'But how—?'

He lifted the corner of the gay scarf bound round the girl's head, so that Mrs Oliver could see the ends of the clothes line.

'Just like *my* murder,' said Mrs Oliver unsteadily. 'But *who*? And *why*?'

'That is the question,' said Poirot.

He forebore to add that those had also been her questions.

And that the answers to them could not be her answers, since the victim was not the Yugoslavian first wife of an Atom Scientist, but Marlene Tucker, a fourteen-year-old village girl who, as far as was known, had not an enemy in the world.

CHAPTER 7

Detective-Inspector Bland sat behind a table in the study. Sir George had met him on arrival, had taken him down to the boathouse and had now returned with him to the house. Down at the boathouse a photographic unit was now busy and the fingerprint men and the medical officer had just arrived.

'This do for you here all right?' asked Sir George.

'Very nicely, thank you, sir.'

'What am I to do about this show that's going on, tell 'em about it, stop it, or what?'

Inspector Bland considered for a moment or two.

'What have you done so far, Sir George?' he asked.

'Haven't said anything. There's a sort of idea floating round that there's been an accident. Nothing more than that. I don't think anyone's suspected yet that it's—er—well, murder.'

'Then leave things as they are just for the moment,' decided Bland. 'The news will get round fast enough, I dare say,' he added cynically. He thought again for a moment or two before asking, 'How many people do you think there are at this affair?'

'Couple of hundred I should say,' answered Sir George, 'and more pouring in every moment. People seem to have come from a good long way round. In fact the whole thing's being a roaring success. Damned unfortunate.'

Inspector Bland inferred correctly that it was the murder and not the success of the fête to which Sir George was referring.

'A couple of hundred,' he mused, 'and any one of them, I suppose, could have done it.'

He sighed.

'Tricky,' said Sir George sympathetically. 'But I don't see what reason any one of them could have had. The whole thing seems quite fantastic—don't see who would want to go murdering a girl like that.'

'How much can you tell me about the girl? She was a local girl, I understand?'

'Yes. Her people live in one of the cottages down near the quay. Her father works at one of the local farms— Paterson's, I think.' He added, 'The mother is here at the fête this afternoon. Miss Brewis—that's my secretary, and she can tell you about everything much better than I can— Miss Brewis winkled the woman out and has got her some- where, giving her cups of tea.'

'Quite so,' said the inspector, approvingly. 'I'm not quite clear yet, Sir George, as to the circumstances of all this. What was the girl doing down there in the boathouse? I understand there's some kind of a murder hunt—or treasure hunt, going on.'

Sir George nodded.

'Yes. We all thought it rather a bright idea. Doesn't seem quite so bright now. I think Miss Brewis can probably explain it all to you better than I can. I'll send her to you, shall I? Unless there's anything else you want to know about first.'

'Not at the moment, Sir George. I may have more questions to ask you later. There are people I shall want to see. You, and Lady Stubbs, and the people who discovered the body. One of them, I gather, is the woman novelist who designed this murder hunt as you call it.'

'That's right. Mrs Oliver. Mrs Ariadne Oliver.'

The inspector's eyebrows went up slightly.

'Oh—her!' he said. 'Quite a best-seller. I've read a lot of her books myself.'

'She's a bit upset at present,' said Sir George, 'naturally, I suppose. I'll tell her you'll be wanting her, shall I? I don't know where my wife is. She seems to have disappeared completely from view. Somewhere among the two or three hundred, I suppose—not that she'll be able to tell you much. I mean about the girl or anything like that. Who would you like to see first?'

'I think perhaps your secretary, Miss Brewis, and after that the girl's mother.'

Sir George nodded and left the room.

The local police constable, Robert Hoskins, opened the door for him and shut it after he went out. He then volunteered a statement, obviously intended as a commentary on some of Sir George's remarks.

'Lady Stubbs is a bit wanting,' he said, 'up *here*.' He tapped his forehead. 'That's why he said she wouldn't be much help. Scatty, that's what she is.'

'Did he marry a local girl?'

'No. Foreigner of some sort. Coloured, some say, but I don't think that's so myself.'

Bland nodded. He was silent for a moment, doodling with a pencil on a sheet of paper in front of him. Then he asked a question which was clearly off the record.

'Who did it, Hoskins?' he said.

If anyone did have any ideas as to what had been going on, Bland thought, it would be P.C. Hoskins. Hoskins was a man of inquisitive mind with a great interest in everybody and everything. He had a gossiping wife and that, taken with his position as local constable, provided him with vast stores of information of a personal nature.

'Foreigner, if you ask me. 'Twouldn't be anyone local. The Tuckers is all right. Nice, respectable family. Nine of 'em all told. Two of the older girls is married, one boy in the Navy, the other one's doing his National Service, another girl's over to a hairdresser's at Torquay. There's three younger ones at home, two boys and a girl.' He paused, considering. 'None of 'em's what you'd call bright, but Mrs Tucker keeps her home nice, clean as a pin— youngest of eleven, she was. She's got her old father living with her.'

Bland received this information in silence. Given in

Hoskins' particular idiom, it was an outline of the Tuckers' social position and standing.

'That's why I say it was a foreigner,' continued Hoskins. 'One of those that stop up to the Hostel at Hoodown, likely as not. There's some queer ones among them—and a lot of goings-on. Be surprised, you would, at what I've seen 'em doing in the bushes and the woods! Every bit as bad as what goes on in parked cars along the Common.'

P.C. Hoskins was by this time an absolute specialist on the subject of sexual 'goings-on.' They formed a large portion of his conversation when off duty and having his pint in the Bull and Bear. Bland said:

'I don't think there was anything—well, of that kind. The doctor will tell us, of course, as soon as he's finished his examination.'

'Yes, sir, that'll be up to him, that will. But what I say is, you never know with foreigners. Turn nasty, they can, all in a moment.'

Inspector Bland sighed as he thought to himself that it was not quite as easy as that. It was all very well for Constable Hoskins to put the blame conveniently on 'foreigners.' The door opened and the doctor walked in.

'Done my bit,' he remarked. 'Shall they take her away now? The other outfits have packed up.'

'Sergeant Cottrill will attend to that,' said Bland. 'Well, Doc, what's the finding?'

'Simple and straightforward as it can be,' said the doctor. 'No complications. Garrotted with a piece of clothes line. Nothing could be simpler or easier to do. No struggle of any kind beforehand. I'd say the kid didn't know what was happening to her until it had happened.'

'Any signs of assault?'

'None. No assault, signs of rape, or interference of any kind.'

'Not presumably a sexual crime, then?'

'I wouldn't say so, no.' The doctor added, 'I shouldn't say she'd been a particularly attractive girl.'

'Was she fond of the boys?'

Bland addressed this question to Constable Hoskins.

'I wouldn't say they'd much use for her,' said Constable Hoskins, 'though maybe she'd have liked it if they had.'

'Maybe,' agreed Bland. His mind went back to the pile of comic papers in the boathouse and the idle scrawls on the margin. 'Johnny goes with Kate,' 'Georgie Porgie kisses hikers in the wood.' He thought there had been a little wishful thinking there. On the whole, though, it seemed unlikely that there was a sex angle to Marlene Tucker's death. Although, of course, one never knew... There were always those queer criminal individuals, men with a secret lust to kill, who specialized in immature female victims. One of these might be present in this part of the world during this holiday season. He almost believed that it *must* be so—for otherwise he could really see no reason for so pointless a crime. However, he thought, we're only at the beginning. I'd better see what all these people have to tell me.

'What about time of death?' he asked.

The doctor glanced over at the clock and his own watch.

'Just after half-past five now,' he said. 'Say I saw her about twenty past five—she'd been dead about an hour. Roughly, that is to say. Put it between four o'clock and twenty to five. Let you know if there's anything more after the autopsy.' He added: 'You'll get the proper report with the long words in due course. I'll be off now. I've got some patients to see.'

He left the room and Inspector Bland asked Hoskins to fetch Miss Brewis. His spirits rose a little when Miss Brewis came into the room. Here, as he recognized at once, was efficiency. He would get clear answers to his questions, definite times and no muddle-headedness.

'Mrs Tucker's in my sitting-room,' Miss Brewis said as she sat down. 'I've broken the news to her and given her some tea. She's very upset, naturally. She wanted to see the body but I told her it was much better not. Mr Tucker gets off work at six o'clock and was coming to join his wife here. I told them to look out for him and bring him along when he arrives. The younger children are at the fête still, and someone is keeping an eye on them.'

'Excellent,' said Inspector Bland, with approval. 'I think before I see Mrs Tucker I would like to hear what you and Lady Stubbs can tell me.'

'I don't know where Lady Stubbs is,' said Miss Brewis acidly. 'I rather imagine she got bored with the fête and has wandered off somewhere, but I don't expect she can tell you anything more than I can. What exactly is it that you want to know?'

'I want to know all the details of this murder hunt first

and of how this girl, Marlene Tucker, came to be taking a part in it.'

'That's quite easy.'

Succinctly and clearly Miss Brewis explained the idea of the murder hunt as an original attraction for the fête, the engaging of Mrs Oliver, the well-known novelist, to arrange the matter, and a short outline of the plot.

'Originally,' Miss Brewis explained, 'Mrs Alec Legge was to have taken the part of the victim.'

'Mrs Alec Legge?' queried the inspector.

Constable Hoskins put in an explanatory word.

'She and Mr Legge have the Lawders' cottage, the pink one down by Mill Creek. Came here a month ago, they did. Two or three months they got it for.'

'I see. And Mrs Legge, you say, was to be the original victim? Why was that changed?'

'Well, one evening Mrs Legge told all our fortunes and was so good at it that it was decided we'd have a fortune teller's tent as one of the attractions and that Mrs Legge should put on Eastern dress and be Madame Zuleika and tell fortunes at half a crown a time. I don't think that's really illegal, is it, Inspector? I mean it's usually done at these kind of fêtes?'

Inspector Bland smiled faintly.

'Fortune telling and raffles aren't always taken too seriously, Miss Brewis,' he said. 'Now and then we have to—er—make an example.'

'But usually you're tactful? Well, that's how it was. Mrs Legge agreed to help us that way and so we had to find somebody else to do the body. The local Guides were helping us at the fête, and I think someone suggested that one of the Guides would do quite well.'

'Just who was it who suggested that, Miss Brewis?'

'Really, I don't quite know... I think it may have been Mrs Masterton, the Member's wife. No, perhaps it was Captain Warburton... Really, I can't be sure. But, anyway, it *was* suggested.'

'Is there any reason why this particular girl should have been chosen?'

'N-no, I don't think so. Her people are tenants on the estate, and her mother, Mrs Tucker, sometimes comes to help in the kitchen. I don't know quite why we settled on her. Probably her name came to mind first. We asked her and she seemed quite pleased to do it.'

'She definitely wanted to do it?'

'Oh, yes, I think she was flattered. She was a very moronic kind of girl,' continued Miss Brewis, 'she couldn't have *acted* a part or anything like that. But this was all very simple, and she felt she'd been singled out from the others and was pleased about it.'

'What exactly was it that she had to do?'

'She had to stay in the boathouse. When she heard anyone coming to the door she was to lie down on the floor, put the cord round her neck and sham dead.' Miss Brewis' tones were calm and businesslike. The fact that the girl who was to sham dead had actually been found dead did not at the moment appear to affect her emotionally.

'Rather a boring way for the girl to spend the afternoon

when she might have been at the fête,' suggested Inspector Bland.

'I suppose it was in a way,' said Miss Brewis, 'but one can't have everything, can one? And Marlene did enjoy the idea of being the body. It made her feel important. She had a pile of papers and things to read to keep her amused.'

'And something to eat as well?' said the inspector. 'I noticed there was a tray down there with a plate and glass.'

'Oh, yes, she had a big plate of sweet cakes, and a raspberry fruit drink. I took them down to her myself.'

Bland looked up sharply.

'You took them down to her? When?'

'About the middle of the afternoon.'

'What time exactly? Can you remember?'

Miss Brewis considered a moment.

'Let me see. Children's Fancy Dress was judged, there was a little delay—Lady Stubbs couldn't be found, but Mrs Folliat took her place, so that was all right... Yes, it must have been—I'm almost sure—about five minutes past four that I collected the cakes and the fruit drink.'

'And you took them down to her at the boathouse yourself. What time did you reach there?'

'Oh, it takes about five minutes to go down to the boathouse—about quarter past four, I should think.'

'And at quarter past four Marlene Tucker was alive and well?'

'Yes, of course,' said Miss Brewis, 'and very eager to know how people were getting on with the murder hunt, too. I'm afraid I couldn't tell her. I'd been too busy with the side show on the lawn, but I did know that a lot of people had entered for it. Twenty or thirty to my knowledge. Probably a good many more.'

'How did you find Marlene when you arrived at the boathouse?'

'I've just told you.'

'No, no, I don't mean that. I mean, was she lying on the floor shamming dead when you opened the door?'

'Oh, no,' said Miss Brewis, 'because I called out just before I got there. So she opened the door and I took the tray in and put it on the table.'

'At a quarter past four,' said Bland, writing it down, 'Marlene Tucker was alive and well. You will understand, I'm sure, Miss Brewis, that that is a very important point. You are quite sure of your times?'

'I can't be exactly sure because I didn't look at my watch, but I had looked at it a short time previously and that's as near as I can get.' She added, with a sudden dawning realization of the inspector's point, 'Do you mean that it was soon after—?'

'It can't have been very long after, Miss Brewis.'

'Oh, dear,' said Miss Brewis.

It was a rather inadequate expression, but nevertheless it conveyed well enough Miss Brewis' dismay and concern.

'Now, Miss Brewis, on your way down to the boathouse and on your way back again to the house, did you meet anybody or see anyone near the boathouse?'

Miss Brewis considered.

'No,' she said, 'I didn't meet anyone. I might have, of

course, because the grounds are open to everyone this afternoon. But on the whole, people tend to stay round the lawn and the side shows and all that. They like to go round the kitchen gardens and the greenhouses, but they don't walk through the woodlands as much as I should have thought they would. People tend to herd together very much at these affairs, don't you think so, Inspector?'

The inspector said that that was probably so.

'Though, I think,' said Miss Brewis, with sudden memory, 'that there *was* someone in the Folly.'

'The Folly?'

'Yes. A small white temple arrangement. It was put up just a year or two ago. It's to the right of the path as you go down to the boathouse. There was someone in there. A courting couple, I suspect. Someone was laughing and then someone said, "Hush."'

'You don't know who this courting couple was?'

'I've no idea. You can't see the front of the Folly from the path. The sides and back are enclosed.'

The inspector thought for a moment or two, but it did not seem likely to him that the couple—whoever they were—in the Folly were important. Better find out who they were, perhaps, because they in their turn might have seen someone coming up from or going down to the boathouse.

'And there was no one else on the path? No one at all?' he insisted.

'I see what you're driving at, of course,' said Miss Brewis. 'I can only assure you that I didn't meet anyone. But then, you see, I needn't have. I mean, if there had been anyone on the path who didn't want me to see them, it's the simplest thing in the world just to slip behind some of the rhododendron bushes. The path's ordered on both sides with shrubs and rhododendron bushes. If anyone who had no business to be there heard someone coming along the path, they could slip out of sight in a moment.'

The inspector shifted on to another tack.

'Is there anything you know about this girl yourself, that could help us?' he asked.

'I really know nothing about her,' said Miss Brewis. 'I don't think I'd ever spoken to her until this affair. She's one of the girls I've seen about—I know her vaguely by sight, but that's all.'

'And you know nothing *about* her—nothing that could be helpful?'

'I don't know of any reason why anyone should want to murder her,' said Miss Brewis. 'In fact it seems to me, if you know what I mean, quite impossible that such a thing should have happened. I can only think that to some unbalanced mind, the fact that she was to be the murdered victim might have induced the wish to make her a real victim. But even that sounds very far fetched and silly.'

Bland sighed.

'Oh, well,' he said, 'I suppose I'd better see the mother now.'

Mrs Tucker was a thin, hatchet-faced woman with stringy blonde hair and a sharp nose. Her eyes were reddened with crying, but she had herself in hand now, and was ready to answer the inspector's questions.

'Doesn't seem right that a thing like that should happen,' she said. 'You read of these things in the papers, but that it should happen to our Marlene—'

'I'm very, very sorry about it,' said Inspector Bland gently. 'What I want you to do is to think as hard as you can and tell me if there is anyone who could have had any reason to harm the girl?'

'I've been thinking about that already,' said Mrs Tucker, with a sudden sniff. 'Thought and thought, I have, but I can't get anywhere. Words with the teacher at school Marlene had now and again, and she'd have her quarrels now and again with one of the girls or boys, but nothing serious in any way. There's no one who had a real down on her, nobody who'd do her a mischief.'

'She never talked to you about anyone who might have been an enemy of any kind?'

'She talked silly often, Marlene did, but nothing of that kind. It was all make-up and hair-dos, and what she'd like to do to her face and herself. You know what girls are. Far too young she was, to put on lipstick and all that muck, and her dad told her so, and so did I. But that's what she'd do when she got hold of any money. Buy herself scent and lipsticks and hide them away.'

Bland nodded. There was nothing here that could help him. An adolescent, rather silly girl, her head full of film stars and glamour—there were hundreds of Marlenes.

'What her dad'll say, I don't know,' said Mrs Tucker. 'Coming here any minute he'll be, expecting to enjoy himself. He's a rare shot at the coconuts, he is.'

She broke down suddenly and began to sob.

'If you ask me,' she said, 'it's one of them nasty foreigners up at the Hostel. You never know where you are with foreigners. Nice spoken as most of them are, some of the shirts they wear you wouldn't believe. Shirts with girls on them with these bikinis, as they call them. And all of them sunning themselves here and there with no shirts at all on—it all leads to trouble. That's what I say!'

Still weeping, Mrs Tucker was escorted from the room by Constable Hoskins. Bland reflected that the local verdict seemed to be the comfortable and probably age-long one of attributing every tragic occurrence to unspecified foreigners.

CHAPTER 8

'Got a sharp tongue, she has,' Hoskins said when he returned. 'Nags her husband and bullies her old father. I dare say she's spoke sharp to the girl once or twice and now she's feeling bad about it. Not that girls mind what their mothers say to them. Drops off 'em like water off a duck's back.'

Inspector Bland cut short these general reflections and told Hoskins to fetch Mrs Oliver.

The inspector was slightly startled by the sight of Mrs Oliver. He had not expected anything so voluminous, so purple and in such a state of emotional disturbance.

'I feel awful,' said Mrs Oliver, sinking down in the chair in front of him like a purple blancmange. 'AWFUL,' she added in what were clearly capital letters.

The inspector made a few ambiguous noises, and Mrs Oliver swept on.

'Because, you see, it's *my* murder. I did it!'

For a startled moment Inspector Bland thought that Mrs Oliver was accusing herself of the crime.

'Why I should ever have wanted the Yugoslavian wife of an Atom Scientist to be the victim, I can't imagine,' said Mrs Oliver, sweeping her hands through her elaborate hair-do in a frenzied manner with the result that she looked slightly drunk. 'Absolutely asinine of me. It might just as well have been the second gardener who wasn't what he seemed—and that wouldn't have mattered half as much because, after all, most men can look after themselves. If they can't look after themselves they ought to be able to look after themselves, and in that case I shouldn't have minded so much. Men get killed and nobody minds—I mean, nobody except their wives and sweethearts and children and things like that.'

At this point the inspector entertained unworthy suspicions about Mrs Oliver. This was aided by the faint fragrance of brandy which was wafted towards him. On their return to the house Hercule Poirot had firmly administered to his friend this sovereign remedy for shocks.

'I'm not mad and I'm not drunk,' said Mrs Oliver, intuitively divining his thoughts, 'though I dare say with that man about who thinks I drink like a fish and says everybody says so, you probably think so too.'

'What man?' demanded the inspector, his mind switching from the unexpected introduction of the second gardener into the drama, to the further introduction of an unspecified man.

'Freckles and a Yorkshire accent,' said Mrs Oliver. 'But, as I say, I'm not drunk and I'm not mad. I'm just upset. Thoroughly UPSET,' she repeated, once more resorting to capital letters.

'I'm sure, madam, it must have been most distressing,' said the inspector.

'The awful thing is,' said Mrs Oliver, 'that she *wanted* to be a sex maniac's victim, and now I suppose she was—is—which should I mean?'

'There's no question of a sex maniac,' said the inspector.

'Isn't there?' said Mrs Oliver. 'Well, thank God for that. Or, at least, I don't know. Perhaps she would rather have had it that way. But if he wasn't a sex maniac, why did anybody murder her, Inspector?'

'I was hoping,' said the inspector, 'that you could help me there.'

Undoubtedly, he thought, Mrs Oliver had put her finger on the crucial point. Why should anyone murder Marlene?

'I can't help you,' said Mrs Oliver. 'I can't imagine who could have done it. At least, of course, I can *imagine*—I can imagine anything! That's the trouble with me. I can imagine things now—this minute. I could even make them sound all right, but of course none of them would be true. I mean, she could have been murdered by someone who just likes murdering girls but that's too easy—and, anyway, too much of a coincidence that somebody should be at this fête who wanted to murder a girl. And how would he know that Marlene was in the boathouse? Or she might have known some secret about somebody's love affairs, or she may have seen someone bury a body at night, or she may have recognized somebody who was concealing his identity—or she may have known a secret about where some treasure was buried during the war. Or the man in the

98

launch may have thrown somebody into the river and she saw it from the window of the boathouse—or she may even have got hold of some very important message in secret code and not known what it was herself.'

'Please!' The inspector held up his hand. His head was whirling.

Mrs Oliver stopped obediently. It was clear that she could have gone on in this vein for some time, although it seemed to the inspector that she had already envisaged every possibility, likely or otherwise. Out of the richness of the material presented to him, he seized upon one phrase.

'What did you mean, Mrs Oliver, by the "man in the launch"? Are you just imagining a man in a launch?'

'Somebody told me he'd come in a launch,' said Mrs Oliver. 'I can't remember who. The one we were talking about at breakfast, I mean,' she added.

'Please.' The inspector's tone was now pleading. He had had no idea before what the writers of detective stories were like. He knew that Mrs Oliver had written forty-odd books. It seemed to him astonishing at the moment that she had not written a hundred and forty. He rapped out a peremptory inquiry. 'What *is* all this about a man at breakfast who came in a launch?'

'He didn't come in the launch at breakfast time,' said Mrs Oliver, 'it was a yacht. At least, I don't mean that exactly. It was a letter.'

'Well, what was it?' demanded Bland. 'A yacht or a letter?'

'It was a letter,' said Mrs Oliver, 'to Lady Stubbs. From a cousin in a yacht. And she was frightened,' she ended.

Agatha Christie

'Frightened? What of?'

'Of him, I suppose,' said Mrs Oliver. 'Anybody could see it. She was terrified of him and she didn't want him to come, and I think that's why she's hiding now.'

'Hiding?' said the inspector.

'Well, she isn't about anywhere,' said Mrs Oliver. 'Everyone's been looking for her. And *I* think she's hiding because she's afraid of him and doesn't want to meet him.'

'Who *is* this man?' demanded the inspector.

'You'd better ask M. Poirot,' said Mrs Oliver. 'Because he spoke to him and I haven't. His name's Estaban—no, it isn't, that was in my plot. De Sousa, that's what his name is, Etienne de Sousa.'

But another name had caught the inspector's attention.

'Who did you say?' he asked. 'Mr Poirot?'

'Yes. Hercule Poirot. He was with me when we found the body.'

'Hercule Poirot... I wonder now. Can it be the same man? A Belgian, a small man with a very big moustache?'

'An enormous moustache,' agreed Mrs Oliver. 'Yes. Do you know him?'

'It's a good many years since I met him. I was a young sergeant at the time.'

'You met him on a murder case?'

'Yes, I did. What's *he* doing down here?'

'He was to give away the prizes,' said Mrs Oliver.

There was a momentary hesitation before she gave this answer, but it went unperceived by the inspector.

'And he was with you when you discovered the body,' said Bland. 'H'm, I'd like to talk to him.'

'Shall I get him for you?' Mrs Oliver gathered up her purple draperies hopefully.

'There's nothing more that you can add, madam? Nothing more that you think could help us in any way?'

'I don't think so,' said Mrs Oliver. 'I don't know anything. As I say, I could imagine reasons—'

The inspector cut her short. He had no wish to hear any more of Mrs Oliver's imagined solutions. They were far too confusing.

'Thank you very much, madam,' he said briskly. 'If you'll ask M. Poirot to come and speak to me here I shall be very much obliged to you.'

Mrs Oliver left the room. P.C. Hoskins inquired with interest:

'Who's this Monsieur Poirot, sir?'

'You'd describe him probably as a scream,' said Inspector Bland. 'Kind of music hall parody of a Frenchman, but actually he's a Belgian. But in spite of his absurdities, he's got brains. He must be a fair age now.'

'What about this De Sousa?' asked the constable. 'Think there's anything in that, sir?'

Inspector Bland did not hear the question. He was struck by a fact which, though he had been told it several times, was only now beginning to register.

First it had been Sir George, irritated and alarmed. 'My wife seems to have disappeared. I can't think where she has got to.' Then Miss Brewis, contemptuous: 'Lady Stubbs was not to be found. She'd got bored with the show.' And now Mrs Oliver with her theory that Lady Stubbs was hiding.

'Eh? What?' he asked absently.

Constable Hoskins cleared his throat.

'I was asking you, sir, if you thought there was anything in this business of De Sousa—whoever *he* is.'

Constable Hoskins was clearly delighted at having a specific foreigner rather than foreigners in the mass introduced into the case. But Inspector Bland's mind was running on a different course.

'I want Lady Stubbs,' he said curtly. 'Get hold of her for me. If she isn't about, look for her.'

Hoskins looked slightly puzzled but he left the room obediently. In the doorway he paused and fell back a little to allow Hercule Poirot to enter. He looked back over his shoulder with some interest before closing the door behind him.

'I don't suppose,' said Bland, rising and holding out his hand, 'that you remember me, M. Poirot.'

'But assuredly,' said Poirot. 'It is—now give me a moment, just a little moment. It is the young sergeant—yes, Sergeant Bland whom I met fourteen—no, fifteen years ago.'

'Quite right. What a memory!'

'Not at all. Since you remember me, why should I not remember you?'

It would be difficult, Bland thought, to forget Hercule Poirot, and this not entirely for complimentary reasons.

'So here you are, M. Poirot,' he said. 'Assisting at a murder once again.'

'You are right,' said Poirot. 'I was called down here to assist.'

'Called down to assist?' Bland looked puzzled. Poirot said quickly:

'I mean, I was asked down here to give away the prizes of this murder hunt.'

'So Mrs Oliver told me.'

'She told you nothing else?' Poirot said it with apparent carelessness. He was anxious to discover whether Mrs Oliver had given the inspector any hint of the real motives which had led her to insist on Poirot's journey to Devon.

'Told me nothing else? She never stopped telling me things. Every possible and impossible motive for the girl's murder. She set my head spinning. Phew! What an imagination!'

'She earns her living by her imagination, *mon ami*,' said Poirot dryly.

'She mentioned a man called De Sousa—did she imagine that?'

'No, that is sober fact.'

'There was something about a letter at breakfast and a yacht and coming up the river in a launch. I couldn't make head or tail of it.'

Poirot embarked upon an explanation. He told of the scene at the breakfast table, the letter, Lady Stubbs' headache.

'Mrs Oliver said that Lady Stubbs was frightened. Did you think she was afraid, too?'

'That was the impression she gave me.'

'Afraid of this cousin of hers? Why?'

Poirot shrugged his shoulders.

'I have no idea. All she told me was that he was bad—a bad man. She is, you understand, a little simple. Subnormal.'

'Yes, that seems to be pretty generally known round here. She didn't say why she was afraid of this De Sousa?'

'No.'

'But you think her fear was real?'

'If it was not, then she is a very clever actress,' said Poirot dryly.

'I'm beginning to have some odd ideas about this case,' said Bland. He got up and walked restlessly to and fro. 'It's that cursed woman's fault, I believe.'

'Mrs Oliver's?'

'Yes. She's put a lot of melodramatic ideas into my head.'

'And you think they may be true?'

'Not all of them—naturally—but one or two of them mightn't be as wild as they sounded. It all depends...' He broke off as the door opened to re-admit P.C. Hoskins.

'Don't seem able to find the lady, sir,' he said. 'She's not about anywhere.'

'I know that already,' said Bland irritably. 'I told you to find her.'

'Sergeant Farrell and P.C. Lorimer are searching the grounds, sir,' said Hoskins. 'She's not in the house,' he added.

'Find out from the man who's taking admission tickets at the gate if she's left the place. Either on foot or in a car.'

'Yes, sir.'

Hoskins departed.

'And find out when she was last seen and where,' Bland shouted after him.

'So that is the way your mind is working,' said Poirot.

'It isn't working anywhere yet,' said Bland, 'but I've just woken up to the fact that a lady who ought to be on the premises isn't on the premises! And I want to know why. Tell me what more you know about what's-his-name De Sousa.'

Poirot described his meeting with the young man who had come up the path from the quay.

'He is probably still here at the fête,' he said. 'Shall I tell Sir George that you want to see him?'

'Not for a moment or two,' said Bland. 'I'd like to find out a little more first. When did you yourself last see Lady Stubbs?'

Poirot cast his mind back. He found it difficult to remember exactly. He recalled vague glimpses of her tall, cyclamen-clad figure with the drooping black hat moving about the lawn talking to people, hovering here and there; occasionally he would hear that strange laugh of hers, distinctive amongst the many other confused sounds.

'I think,' he said doubtfully, 'it must have been not long before four o'clock.'

'And where was she then, and who was she with?'

'She was in the middle of a group of people near the house.'

'Was she there when De Sousa arrived?'

'I don't remember. I don't think so, at least I did not see her. Sir George told De Sousa that his wife was some-where about. He seemed surprised, I remember, that she was not judging the Children's Fancy Dress, as she was supposed to do.'

'What time was it when De Sousa arrived?'

'It must have been about half-past four, I should think. I did not look at my watch so I cannot tell you exactly.'

'And Lady Stubbs had disappeared before he arrived?'

'It seems so.'

'Possibly she ran away so as not to meet him,' suggested the inspector.

'Possibly,' Poirot agreed.

'Well, she can't have gone far,' said Bland. 'We ought to be able to find her quite easily, and when we do...' He broke off.

'And supposing you don't?' Poirot put the question with a curious intonation in his voice.

'That's nonsense,' said the inspector vigorously. 'Why? What d'you think's happened to her?'

Poirot shrugged his shoulders.

'What indeed! One does not know. All one does know is that she has—disappeared!'

'Dash it all, M. Poirot, you're making it sound quite sinister.'

'Perhaps it *is* sinister.'

'It's the murder of Marlene Tucker that we're investigating,' said the inspector severely.

'But evidently. So—why this interest in De Sousa? Do you think he killed Marlene Tucker?'

Inspector Bland replied irrelevantly:

'It's that woman!'

Poirot smiled faintly.

'Mrs Oliver, you mean?'

'Yes. You see, M. Poirot, the murder of Marlene Tucker doesn't make sense. It doesn't make sense at all. Here's a nondescript, rather moronic kid found strangled and not a hint of any possible motive.'

'And Mrs Oliver supplied you with a motive?'

'With a dozen at least! Amongst them she suggested that Marlene might have a knowledge of somebody's secret love affair, or that Marlene might have witnessed somebody being murdered, or that she knew where a buried treasure was hidden, or that she might have seen from the window of the boathouse some action performed by De Sousa in his launch as he was going up the river.'

'Ah. And which of those theories appeals to you, *mon cher*?'

'I don't know. But I can't help thinking about them. Listen, M. Poirot. Think back carefully. Would you say from your impression of what Lady Stubbs said to you this morning that she was afraid of her cousin's coming because he might, perhaps, know something about her which she did not want to come to the ears of her husband, or would you say that it was a direct personal fear of the man himself?'

Poirot had no hesitation in his reply.

'I should say it was a direct personal fear of the man himself.'

'H'm,' said Inspector Bland. 'Well, I'd better have a little talk with this young man if he's still about the place.'

CHAPTER 9

Although he had none of Constable Hoskins' ingrained prejudice against foreigners, Inspector Bland took an instant dislike to Etienne de Sousa. The polished elegance of the young man, his sartorial perfection, the rich flowery smell of his brilliantined hair, all combined to annoy the inspector.

De Sousa was very sure of himself, very much at ease. He also displayed, decorously veiled, a certain aloof amusement.

'One must admit,' he said, 'that life is full of surprises. I arrive here on a holiday cruise, I admire the beautiful scenery, I come to spend an afternoon with a little cousin that I have not seen for years—and what happens? First I am engulfed in a kind of carnival with coconuts whizzing past my head, and immediately afterwards, passing from comedy to tragedy, I am embroiled in a murder.'

He lit a cigarette, inhaled deeply, and said:

'Not that it concerns me in any way, this murder. Indeed, I am at a loss to know why you should want to interview me.'

'You arrived here as a stranger, Mr De Sousa—'

De Sousa interrupted:

'And strangers are necessarily suspicious, is that it?'

'No, no, not at all, sir. No, you don't take my meaning. Your yacht, I understand, is moored in Helmmouth?'

'That is so, yes.'

'And you came up the river this afternoon in a motor launch?'

'Again—that is so.'

'As you came up the river, did you notice on your right a small boathouse jutting out into the river with a thatched roof and a little mooring quay underneath it?'

De Sousa threw back his handsome, dark head and frowned as he reflected.

'Let me see, there was a creek and a small grey tiled house.'

'Farther up the river than that, Mr De Sousa. Set amongst trees.'

'Ah, yes, I remember now. A very picturesque spot. I did not know it was the boathouse attached to this house. If I had done so, I would have moored my boat there and come ashore. When I asked for directions I had been told to come up to the ferry itself and go ashore at the quay there.'

'Quite so. And that is what you did?'

'That is what I did.'

'You didn't land at, or near, the boathouse?'

De Sousa shook his head.

'Did you see anyone at the boathouse as you passed?'

'See anyone? No. Should I have seen anyone?'

'It was just a possibility. You see, Mr De Sousa, the murdered girl was in the boathouse this afternoon. She was killed there, and she must have been killed at a time not very distant from when you were passing.'

Again De Sousa raised his eyebrows.

'You think I might have been a witness to this murder?'

'The murder took place inside the boathouse, but you might have seen the girl—she might have looked out from the window or come out on to the balcony. If you had seen her it would, at any rate, have narrowed the time of death for us. If, when you'd passed, she'd been still alive—'

'Ah. I see. Yes, I see. But why ask *me* particularly? There are plenty of boats going up and down from Helmmouth. Pleasure steamers. They pass the whole time. Why not ask them?'

'We shall ask them,' said the inspector. 'Never fear, we shall ask them. I am to take it, then, that you saw nothing unusual at the boathouse?'

'Nothing whatever. There was nothing to show there was anyone there. Of course I did not look at it with any special attention, and I did not pass very near. Somebody might have been looking out of the windows, as you suggest, but if so I should not have seen that person.' He added in a polite tone, 'I am very sorry that I cannot assist you.'

'Oh, well,' said Inspector Bland in a friendly manner, 'we

can't hope for too much. There are just a few other things I would like to know, Mr De Sousa.'

'Yes?'

'Are you alone down here or have you friends with you on this cruise?'

'I have had friends with me until quite recently, but for the last three days I have been on my own—with the crew, of course.'

'And the name of your yacht, Mr De Sousa?'

'The *Espérance*.'

'Lady Stubbs is, I understand, a cousin of yours?'

De Sousa shrugged his shoulders.

'A distant cousin. Not very near. In the islands, you must understand, there is much inter-marrying. We are all cousins of one another. Hattie is a second or third cousin. I have not seen her since she was practically a little girl, fourteen—fifteen.'

'And you thought you would pay her a surprise visit today?'

'Hardly a *surprise* visit, Inspector. I had already written to her.'

'I know that she received a letter from you this morning, but it was a surprise to her to know that you were in this country.'

'Oh, but you are wrong there, Inspector. I wrote to my cousin—let me see, three weeks ago. I wrote to her from France just before I came across to this country.'

The inspector was surprised.

'You wrote to her from France telling her you proposed to visit her?'

'Yes. I told her I was going on a yachting cruise and that we should probably arrive at Torquay or Helmmouth round about this date, and that I would let her know later exactly when I should arrive.'

Inspector Bland stared at him. This statement was at complete variance with what he had been told about the arrival of Etienne de Sousa's letter at the breakfast table. More than one witness had testified to Lady Stubbs having been alarmed and upset and very clearly startled at the contents of the letter. De Sousa returned his stare calmly. With a little smile he flicked a fragment of dust from his knee.

'Did Lady Stubbs reply to your first letter?' the inspector asked.

De Sousa hesitated for a moment or two before he answered, then he said:

'It is so difficult to remember... No, I do not think she did. But it was not necessary. I was travelling about, I had no fixed address. And besides, I do not think my cousin, Hattie, is very good at writing letters.' He added: 'She is not, you know, very intelligent, though I understand that she has grown into a very beautiful woman.'

'You have not yet seen her?' Bland put it in the form of a question and De Sousa showed his teeth in an agreeable smile.

'She seems to be most unaccountably missing,' he said. 'No doubt this *espèce de gala* bores her.'

Choosing his words carefully, Inspector Bland said:

'Have you any reason to believe, Mr De Sousa, that your cousin might have some reason for wishing to avoid you?'

'Hattie wish to avoid me? Really, I do not see why. What reason could she have?'

'That is what I am asking you, Mr De Sousa.'

'You think that Hattie has absented herself from this fête in order to avoid me? What an absurd idea.'

'She had no reason, as far as you know, to be—shall we say—afraid of you in any way?'

'Afraid—of *me*?' De Sousa's voice was sceptical and amused. 'But if I may say so, Inspector, what a fantastic idea!'

'Your relations with her have always been quite amicable?'

'It is as I have told you. I have had no relations with her. I have not seen her since she was a child of fourteen.'

'Yet you look her up when you come to England?'

'Oh, as to that, I had seen a paragraph about her in one of your society papers. It mentions her maiden name and that she is married to this rich Englishman, and I think "I must see what the little Hattie has turned into. Whether her brains now work better than they used to do."' He shrugged his shoulders again. 'It was a mere cousinly politeness. A gentle curiosity—no more.'

Again the inspector stared hard at De Sousa. What, he wondered, was going on behind the mocking, smooth façade? He adopted a more confidential manner.

'I wonder if you can perhaps tell me a little more about your cousin? Her character, her reactions?'

De Sousa appeared politely surprised.

'Really—has this anything to do with the murder of the

113

girl in the boathouse, which I understand is the real matter with which you occupy yourself?'

'It might have a connection,' said Inspector Bland.

De Sousa studied him for a moment or two in silence. Then he said with a slight shrug of the shoulders:

'I never knew my cousin at all well. She was a unit in a large family and not particularly interesting to me. But in answer to your question I would say to you that although mentally weak, she was not, as far as I know, ever possessed by any homicidal tendencies.'

'Really, Mr De Sousa, I wasn't suggesting that!'

'Weren't you? I wonder. I can see no other reason for your question. No, unless Hattie has changed very much, she is not homicidal!' He rose. 'I am sure that you cannot want to ask me anything further, Inspector. I can only wish you every possible success in tracking down the murderer.'

'You are not thinking of leaving Helmmouth for a day or two, I hope, Mr De Sousa?'

'You speak very politely, Inspector. Is that an order?'

'Just a request, sir.'

'Thank you. I propose to stay in Helmmouth for two days. Sir George has very kindly asked me to come and stay in the house, but I prefer to remain on the *Espérance*. If you should want to ask me any further questions, that is where you will find me.'

He bowed politely.

P.C. Hoskins opened the door for him, and he went out.

'Smarmy sort of fellow,' muttered the inspector to himself.

'Aah,' said P.C. Hoskins in complete agreement.

'Say she *is* homicidal if you like,' went on the inspector, to himself. 'Why should she attack a nondescript girl? There'd be no sense in it.'

'You never know with the barmy ones,' said Hoskins.

'The question really is, how barmy is she?'

Hoskins shook his head sapiently.

'Got a low I.Q., I reckon,' he said.

The inspector looked at him with annoyance.

'Don't bring out these new-fangled terms like a parrot. I don't care if she's got a high I.Q. or a low I.Q. All I care about is, is she the sort of woman who'd think it funny, or desirable, or necessary, to put a cord round a girl's neck and strangle her? And where the devil *is* the woman, anyway? Go out and see how Frank's getting on.'

Hoskins left obediently, and returned a moment or two later with Sergeant Cottrell, a brisk young man with a good opinion of himself, who always managed to annoy his superior officer. Inspector Bland much preferred the rural wisdom of Hoskins to the smart know-all attitude of Frank Cottrell.

'Still searching the grounds, sir,' said Cottrell. 'The lady hasn't passed out through the gate, we're quite sure of that. It's the second gardener who's there giving out the tickets and taking the admission money. He'll swear she hasn't left.'

'There are other ways of leaving than by the main gate, I suppose?'

'Oh, yes, sir. There's the path down to the ferry, but the old boy down there—Merdell, his name is—is also quite positive that she hasn't left that way. He's about a hundred, but pretty reliable, I think. He described quite clearly how the foreign gentleman arrived in his launch and asked the way to Nasse House. The old man told him he must go up the road to the gate and pay for admission. But he said the gentleman seemed to know nothing about the fête and said he was a relation of the family. So the old man set him on the path up from the ferry through the woods. Merdell seems to have been hanging about the quay all the afternoon so he'd be pretty sure to have seen her ladyship if she'd come that way. Then there's the top gate that leads over the fields to Hoodown Park, but that's been wired up because of trespassers, so she didn't go through there. Seems as though she must be still here, doesn't it?'

'That may be so,' said the inspector, 'but there's nothing to prevent her, is there, from slipping under a fence and going off across country? Sir George is still complaining of trespassing here from the hostel next door, I understand. If you can get in the way the trespassers get in, you can get out the same way, I suppose.'

'Oh, yes, sir, indubitably, sir. But I've talked to her maid, sir. She's wearing'—Cottrell consulted a paper in his hand—'a dress of cyclamen crêpe georgette (whatever that is), a large black hat, black court shoes with four-inch french heels. Not the sort of things you'd wear for a cross-country run.'

'She didn't change her clothes?'

'No. I went into that with the maid. There's nothing missing—nothing whatever. She didn't pack a suitcase or anything of that kind. She didn't even change her shoes. Every pair's there and accounted for.'

Inspector Bland frowned. Unpleasant possibilities were rising in his mind. He said curtly:

'Get me that secretary woman again—Bruce—whatever her name is.'

II

Miss Brewis came in looking rather more ruffled than usual, and a little out of breath.

'Yes, Inspector?' she said. 'You wanted me? If it isn't urgent, Sir George is in a terrible state and—'

'What's he in a state about?'

'He's only just realized that Lady Stubbs is—well, really missing. I told him she's probably only gone for a walk in the woods or something, but he's got it into his head that something's happened to her. *Quite* absurd.'

'It might not be so absurd, Miss Brewis. After all, we've had one—murder here this afternoon.'

'You surely don't think that Lady Stubbs—? But that's ridiculous! Lady Stubbs can look after herself.'

'Can she?'

'Of course she can! She's a grown woman, isn't she?'

'But rather a helpless one, by all accounts.'

'Nonsense,' said Miss Brewis. 'It suits Lady Stubbs now and then to play the helpless nitwit if she doesn't want to do anything. It takes her husband in, I dare say, but it doesn't take *me* in!'

'You don't like her very much, Miss Brewis?' Bland sounded gently interested.

Miss Brewis' lips closed in a thin line.

'It's not my business either to like or dislike her,' she said.

The door burst open and Sir George came in.

'Look here,' he said violently, 'you've got to do something. Where's Hattie? You've got to find Hattie. What the hell's going on round here I don't know. This confounded fête—some ruddy homicidal maniac's got in here, paying his half-crown and looking like everyone else, spending his afternoon going round murdering people. That's what it looks like to me.'

'I don't think we need take such an exaggerated view as that, Sir George.'

'It's all very well for you sitting there behind the table, writing things down. What I want is my wife.'

'I'm having the grounds searched, Sir George.'

'Why did nobody tell me she'd disappeared? She's been missing a couple of hours now, it seems. I thought it was odd that she didn't turn up to judge the Children's Fancy Dress stuff, but nobody told me she'd really gone.'

'Nobody knew,' said the inspector.

'Well, someone ought to've known. Somebody ought to have noticed.'

He turned on Miss Brewis.

'You ought to have known, Amanda, you were keeping an eye on things.'

'I can't be everywhere,' said Miss Brewis. She sounded suddenly almost tearful. 'I've got so much to see to. If Lady Stubbs chose to wander away—'

'Wander away? Why should she wander away? She'd no reason to wander away unless she wanted to avoid that dago fellow.'

Bland seized his opportunity.

'There is something I want to ask you,' he said. 'Did your wife receive a letter from Mr De Sousa some three weeks ago, telling her he was coming to this country?'

Sir George looked astonished.

'No, of course she didn't.'

'You're sure of that?'

'Oh, quite sure. Hattie would have told me. Why, she was thoroughly startled and upset when she got his letter this morning. It more or less knocked her out. She was lying down most of the morning with a headache.'

'What did she say to you privately about her cousin's visit? Why did she dread seeing him so much?'

Sir George looked rather embarrassed.

'Blessed if I really know,' he said. 'She just kept saying that he was wicked.'

'Wicked? In what way?'

'She wasn't very articulate about it. Just went on rather like a child saying that he was a wicked man. Bad; and that she wished he wasn't coming here. She said he'd done bad things.'

'Done bad things? When?'

'Oh, long ago. I should imagine this Etienne de Sousa was the black sheep of the family and that Hattie picked up odds and ends about him during her childhood without understanding them very well. And as a result she's got a sort of horror of him. I thought it was just a childish hangover myself. My wife *is* rather childish sometimes. Has likes and dislikes, but can't explain them.'

'You are sure she did not particularize in any way, Sir George?'

Sir George looked uneasy.

'I wouldn't want you to go by—er—what she said.'

'Then she did say something?'

'All right. I'll let you have it. What she said was—and she said it several times—"*He kills people.*"'

CHAPTER 10

'He kills people,' Inspector Bland repeated.

'I don't think you ought to take it too seriously,' said Sir George. 'She kept repeating it and saying, "He kills people," but she couldn't tell me who he killed or when or why. I thought myself it was just some queer, child-like memory—trouble with the natives—something like that.'

'You say she couldn't tell you anything definite—do you mean *couldn't*, Sir George—or might it have been *wouldn't*?'

'I don't think...' He broke off. 'I don't know. You've muddled me. As I say, I didn't take any of it seriously. I thought perhaps this cousin had teased her a bit when she was a kid—something of that kind. It's difficult to explain to you because you don't know my wife. I am devoted to her, but half the time I don't listen to what she says because it just doesn't make sense. Anyway, this De Sousa fellow

121

couldn't have had anything to do with all this—don't tell me he lands here off a yacht and goes straightaway through the woods and kills a wretched Girl Guide in a boathouse! Why should he?'

'I'm not suggesting that anything like that happened,' said Inspector Bland, 'but you must realize, Sir George, that in looking for the murderer of Marlene Tucker the field is a more restricted one than one might think at first.'

'Restricted!' Sir George stared. 'You've got the whole ruddy fête to choose from, haven't you? Two hundred—three hundred—people? Any one of 'em might have done it.'

'Yes, I thought so at first, but from what I've learnt now that's hardly so. The boathouse door has a Yale lock. Nobody could come in from outside without a key.'

'Well, there were three keys.'

'Exactly. One key was the final clue in this Murder Hunt. It is still concealed in the hydrangea walk at the very top of the garden. The second key was in the possession of Mrs Oliver, the organizer of the Murder Hunt. Where is the third key, Sir George?'

'It ought to be in the drawer of that desk where you're sitting. No, the right-hand one with a lot of the other estate duplicates.'

He came over and rummaged in the drawer.

'Yes. Here it is all right.'

'Then you see,' said Inspector Bland, 'what that means? The only people who could have got into the boathouse

122

were first, the person who had completed the Murder Hunt and found the key (which as far as we know, did not happen). Second, Mrs Oliver or some member of the household to whom she may have lent her key, and, third, someone *whom Marlene herself admitted to the room.*'

'Well, that latter point covers pretty well everyone, doesn't it?'

'Very far from it,' said Inspector Bland. 'If I understand the arrangement of this Murder Hunt correctly, when the girl heard anyone approaching the door she was to lie down and enact the part of the Victim, and wait to be discovered by the person who had found the last clue— the key. Therefore, as you must see for yourself, the only people whom she would have admitted, had they called to her from outside and asked her to do so, *were the people who had actually arranged the Murder Hunt*. Any inmate, that is, of this house—that is to say, yourself, Lady Stubbs, Miss Brewis, Mrs Oliver—possibly M. Poirot whom I believe she had met this morning. Who else, Sir George?'

Sir George considered for a moment or two.

'The Legges, of course,' he said. 'Alec and Sally Legge. They've been in it from the start. And Michael Weyman, he's an architect staying here in the house to design a tennis pavilion. And Warburton, the Mastertons—oh, and Mrs Folliat of course.'

'That is all—nobody else?'

'That's the lot.'

'So you see, Sir George, it is not a very wide field.'

Sir George's face went scarlet.

'I think you're talking nonsense—absolute nonsense! Are you suggesting—what you are suggesting?'

'I'm only suggesting,' said Inspector Bland, 'that there's a great deal we don't know as yet. It's possible, for instance, that Marlene, for some reason, came *out* of the boathouse. She may even have been strangled somewhere else, and her body brought back and arranged on the floor. But even if so, whoever arranged her was again someone who was thoroughly cognisant with all the details of the Murder Hunt. We always come back to that.' He added in a slightly changed voice, 'I can assure you, Sir George, that we're doing all we can to find Lady Stubbs. In the meantime I'd like to have a word with Mr and Mrs Alec Legge and Mr Michael Weyman.'

'Amanda.'

'I'll see what I can do about it, Inspector,' said Miss Brewis. 'I expect Mrs Legge is still telling fortunes in the tent. A lot of people have come in with the half-price admission since five o'clock, and all the side shows are busy. I can probably get hold of Mr Legge or Mr Weyman for you—whichever you want to see first.'

'It doesn't matter in what order I see them,' said Inspector Bland.

Miss Brewis nodded and left the room. Sir George followed her, his voice rising plaintively.

'Look here, Amanda, you've got to...'

Inspector Bland realized that Sir George depended a great

deal upon the efficient Miss Brewis. Indeed, at this moment, Bland found the master of the house rather like a small boy.

Whilst waiting, Inspector Bland picked up the telephone, demanded to be put through to the police station at Helmmouth and made certain arrangements with them concerning the yacht *Espérance*.

'You realize, I suppose,' he said to Hoskins, who was obviously quite incapable of realizing anything of the sort, 'that there's just one perfectly possible place where this damn' woman might be—and that's on board De Sousa's yacht?'

'How d'you make that out, sir?'

'Well, the woman has not been seen to leave by any of the usual exits, she's togged up in a way that makes it unlikely that she's legging it through the fields or woods, but it *is* just possible that she met De Sousa by appointment down at the boathouse and that he took her by launch to the yacht, returning to the fête afterwards.'

'And why would he do that, sir?' demanded Hoskins, puzzled.

'I've no idea,' said the inspector, 'and it's very unlikely that he did. But it's a *possibility*. And if she *is* on the *Espérance*, I'll see to it that she won't get off there without being observed.'

'But if her fair hated the sight of him...' Hoskins dropped into the vernacular.

'All we know is that she *said* she did. Women,' said the

inspector sententiously, 'tell a lot of lies. Always remember that, Hoskins.'

'Aah,' said Constable Hoskins appreciatively.

II

Further conversation was brought to an end as the door opened and a tall vague-looking young man entered. He was wearing a neat grey flannel suit, but his shirt collar was crumpled and his tie askew and his hair stood up on end in an unruly fashion.

'Mr Alec Legge?' said the inspector, looking up.

'No,' said the young man, 'I'm Michael Weyman. You asked for me, I understand.'

'Quite true, sir,' said Inspector Bland. 'Won't you take a chair?' He indicated a chair at the opposite side of the table.

'I don't care for sitting,' said Michael Weyman, 'I like to stride about. What are all you police doing here anyway? What's happened?'

Inspector Bland looked at him in surprise.

'Didn't Sir George inform you, sir?' he asked.

'Nobody's "informed me," as you put it, of anything. I don't sit in Sir George's pocket all the time. What *has* happened?'

'You're staying in the house, I understand?'

'Of course I'm staying in the house. What's that got to do with it?'

'Simply that I imagined that all the people staying in the

126

house would by now have been informed of this afternoon's tragedy.'

'Tragedy? What tragedy?'

'The girl who was playing the part of the murder victim has been killed.'

'No!' Michael Weyman seemed exuberantly surprised. 'Do you mean really killed? No fakery-pokery?'

'I don't know what you mean by fakery-pokery. The girl's dead.'

'How was she killed?'

'Strangled with a piece of cord.'

Michael Weyman gave a whistle.

'Exactly as in the scenario? Well, well, that does give one ideas.' He strode over to the window, turned rapidly about, and said, 'So we're all under suspicion, are we? Or was it one of the local boys?'

'We don't see how it could possibly have been one of the local boys, as you put it,' said the inspector.

'No more do I really,' said Michael Weyman. 'Well, Inspector, many of my friends call me crazy, but I'm not that kind of crazy. I don't roam around the countryside strangling under-developed spotty young women.'

'You are down here, I understand, Mr Weyman, designing a tennis pavilion for Sir George?'

'A blameless occupation,' said Michael. 'Criminally speaking, that is. Architecturally, I'm not so sure. The finished product will probably represent a crime against good taste. But that doesn't interest you, Inspector. What *does* interest you?'

'Well, I should like to know, Mr Weyman, exactly where you were between quarter past four this afternoon and say five o'clock.'

'How do you tape it down to that—medical evidence?'

'Not entirely, sir. A witness saw the girl alive at a quarter past four.'

'What witness—or mayn't I ask?'

'Miss Brewis. Lady Stubbs asked her to take down a tray of creamy cakes with some fruitade to the girl.'

'Our Hattie asked her that? I don't believe it for a moment.'

'Why don't you believe it, Mr Weyman?'

'It's not like her. Not the sort of thing she'd think of or bother about. Dear Lady Stubbs' mind revolves entirely round herself.'

'I'm still waiting, Mr Weyman, for your answer to my question.'

'Where I was between four-fifteen and five o'clock? Well, really, Inspector, I can't say off-hand. I was about—if you know what I mean.'

'About where?'

'Oh, here and there. I mingled a bit on the lawn, watched the locals amusing themselves, had a word or two with the fluttery film star. Then, when I got sick of it all, I went along to the tennis court and mused over the design for the Pavilion. I also wondered how soon someone would identify the photograph that was the first clue for the Murder Hunt with a section of tennis net.'

'Did someone identify it?'

'Yes, I believe someone did come along, but I wasn't really noticing by then. I got a new idea about the Pavilion—a way of making the best of two worlds. My own and Sir George's.'

'And after that?'

'After that? Well, I strolled around and came back to the house. I strolled down the quay and had a crack with old Merdell, then came back. I can't fix any of the times with any accuracy. I was, as I said, in the first place, *about*! That's all there is to it.'

'Well, Mr Weyman,' said the inspector briskly, 'I expect we can get some confirmation of all this.'

'Merdell can tell you that I talked to him on the quay. But of course that'll be rather later than the time you're interested in. Must have been after five when I got down there. Very unsatisfactory, isn't it, Inspector?'

'We shall be able to narrow it down, I expect, Mr Weyman.'

The inspector's tone was pleasant, but there was a steely ring in it that did not escape the young architect's notice. He sat down on the arm of a chair.

'Seriously,' he said, 'who can have wanted to murder that girl?'

'You've no ideas yourself, Mr Weyman?'

'Well, off-hand, I'd say it was our prolific authoress, the Purple Peril. Have you seen her imperial purple getup? I suggest that she went a bit off her onion and thought how much better the Murder Hunt would be if there was a *real* body. How's that?'

'Is that a serious suggestion, Mr Weyman?'

'It's the only probability I can think of.'

'There's one other thing I would like to ask you, Mr Weyman. Did you see Lady Stubbs during the course of the afternoon?'

'Of course I saw her. Who could miss her? Dressed up like a mannequin of Jacques Fath or Christian Dior?'

'When did you see her last?'

'Last? I don't know. Striking an attitude on the lawn about half-past three—or a quarter to four perhaps.'

'And you didn't see her after that?'

'No. Why?'

'I wondered—because after four o'clock nobody seems to have seen her. Lady Stubbs has—vanished, Mr Weyman.'

'Vanished! Our Hattie?'

'That surprises you?'

'Yes, it does rather... What's she up to, I wonder?'

'D'you know Lady Stubbs well, Mr Weyman?'

'Never met her till I came down here four or five days ago.'

'Have you formed any opinions about her?'

'I should say she knows which side her bread is buttered better than most,' said Michael Weyman dryly. 'A very ornamental young woman and knows how to make the most of it.'

'But mentally not very active? Is that right?'

'Depends what you mean by mentally,' said Michael

130

Weyman. 'I wouldn't describe her as an intellectual. But if you're thinking that she's not all there, you're wrong.' A tone of bitterness came into his voice. 'I'd say she was very much all there. Nobody more so.'

The inspector's eyebrows rose.

'That's not the generally accepted opinion.'

'For some reason she likes playing the dim nitwit. I don't know why. But as I've said before, in my opinion, she's very much all there.'

The inspector studied him for a moment, then he said:

'And you really can't get any nearer to exact times and places between the hours I have mentioned?'

'Sorry.' Weyman spoke jerkily. 'I'm afraid I can't. Rotten memory, never any good about time.' He added, 'Finished with me?'

As the inspector nodded, he left the room quickly.

'And I'd like to know,' said the inspector, half to himself and half to Hoskins, 'what there's been between him and her Ladyship. Either he's made a pass at her and she's turned him down, or there's been some kind of a dust-up.' He went on, 'What would you say was the general opinion round these parts about Sir George and his lady?'

'She's daft,' said Constable Hoskins.

'I know *you* think that, Hoskins. Is that the accepted view?'

'I'd say so.'

'And Sir George—is he liked?'

'He's liked well enough. He's a good sportsman and he

knows a bit about farming. The old lady's done a lot to help.'

'What old lady?'

'Mrs Folliat who lives at the Lodge here.'

'Oh, of course. The Folliats used to own this place, didn't they?'

'Yes, and it's owing to the old lady that Sir George and Lady Stubbs have been taken up as well as they have. Got 'em in with the nobs everywhere, she has.'

'Paid for doing so, do you think?'

'Oh, no, not Mrs Folliat.' Hoskins sounded shocked. 'I understand she knew Lady Stubbs before she was married and it was she who urged on Sir George to buy this place.'

'I'll have to talk to Mrs Folliat,' said the inspector.

'Ah, she's a shrewd old lady, she is. If anything is going on, she'd know about it.'

'I must talk to her,' said the inspector. 'I wonder where she is now.'

CHAPTER 11

Mrs Folliat was at that moment being talked to by Hercule Poirot in the big drawing-room. He had found her there leaning back in a chair in a corner of the room. She had started nervously when he came in. Then sinking back, she had murmured:

'Oh, it's you, M. Poirot.'

'I apologize, Madame. I disturbed you.'

'No, no. You don't disturb me. I'm just resting, that's all. I'm not as young as I was. The shock—it was too much for me.'

'I comprehend,' said Poirot. 'Indeed, I comprehend.'

Mrs Folliat, a handkerchief clutched in her small hand, was staring up at the ceiling. She said in a voice half-stifled with emotion:

'I can hardly bear to think of it. That poor girl. That poor, poor girl—'

'I know,' said Poirot. 'I know.'

'So young,' said Mrs Folliat; 'just at the beginning of life.' She said again, 'I can hardly bear to think of it.'

Poirot looked at her curiously. She seemed, he thought,

to have aged by about ten years since the time early in the afternoon, when he had seen her, the gracious hostess, welcoming her guests. Now her face seemed drawn and haggard with the lines in it clearly marked.

'You said to me only yesterday, Madame, it is a very wicked world.'

'Did I say that?' Mrs Folliat seemed startled. 'It's true... Oh, yes, I'm only just beginning to know how true it is.' She added in a low voice, 'But I never thought anything like this would happen.'

Again he looked at her curiously.

'What did you think would happen, then? Something?'

'No, no. I didn't mean that.'

Poirot persisted.

'But you did expect *something* to happen—something out of the usual.'

'You misunderstand me, M. Poirot. I only mean that it's the last thing you would expect to happen in the middle of a fête like this.'

'Lady Stubbs this morning also spoke of wickedness.'

'Hattie did? Oh, don't speak of her to me—don't speak of her. I don't want to think about her.' She was silent for a moment or two, and then said, 'What did she say—about wickedness?'

'She was speaking of her cousin. Etienne de Sousa. She said that he was wicked, that he was a bad man. She said, too, that she was afraid of him.'

He watched, but she merely shook her head incredulously.

'Etienne de Sousa—who is he?'

'Of course, you were not at breakfast. I forgot, Mrs Folliat. Lady Stubbs received a letter from this cousin of hers whom she had not seen since she was a girl of fifteen. He told her that he proposed to call upon her today, this afternoon.'

'And did he come?'

'Yes. He arrived here about half-past four.'

'Surely—d'you mean that rather handsome, dark young man who came up the ferry path? I wondered who he was at the time.'

'Yes, Madame, that was Mr De Sousa.'

Mrs Folliat said energetically:

'If I were you I should pay no attention to the things Hattie says.' She flushed as Poirot looked at her in surprise and went on, 'She is like a child—I mean, she uses terms like a child— wicked, good. No half shades. I shouldn't pay any attention to what she tells you about this Etienne de Sousa.'

Again Poirot wondered. He said slowly:

'You know Lady Stubbs very well, do you not, Mrs Folliat?'

'Probably as well as anyone knows her. Possibly even better than her husband really knows her. And if I do?'

'What is she really like, Madame?'

'What a very odd question, M. Poirot.'

'You know, do you not, Madame, that Lady Stubbs cannot be found anywhere?'

Again her answer surprised him. She expressed no concern or astonishment. She said:

'So she has run away, has she? I see.'

'It seems to you quite natural, that?'

'Natural? Oh, I don't know. Hattie is rather unaccountable.'

'Do you think she has run away because she has a guilty conscience?'

'What do you mean, M. Poirot?'

'Her cousin was talking about her this afternoon. He mentioned casually that she had always been mentally subnormal. I think you must know, Madame, that people who are subnormal mentally are not always accountable for their actions.'

'What are you trying to say, M. Poirot?'

'Such people are, as you say, very simple—like children. In a sudden fit of rage they might even kill.'

Mrs Folliat turned on him in sudden anger.

'Hattie was never like that! I won't allow you to say such things. She was a gentle warm-hearted girl, even if she was—a little simple mentally. Hattie would never have killed *anyone*.'

She faced him, breathing hard, still indignant.

Poirot wondered. He wondered very much.

II

Breaking into this scene, P.C. Hoskins made his appearance.

He said in an apologetic manner:

'I've been looking for you, ma'am.'

'Good evening, Hoskins.' Mrs Folliat was once more her

poised self again, the mistress of Nasse House. 'Yes, what is it?'

'The inspector's compliments, and he'd be glad to have a word with you—if you feels up to it, that is,' Hoskins hastened to add; noting, as Hercule Poirot had done, the effects of shock.

'Of course I feel up to it.' Mrs Folliat rose to her feet. She followed Hoskins out of the room. Poirot, having risen politely, sat down again and stared up at the ceiling with a puzzled frown.

The inspector rose when Mrs Folliat entered and the constable held the chair for her to sit down.

'I'm sorry to worry you, Mrs Folliat,' said Bland. 'But I imagine that you know all the people in the neighbourhood and I think you may be able to help us.'

Mrs Folliat smiled faintly. 'I expect,' she said, 'that I know everyone round here as well as anyone could do. What do you want to know, Inspector?'

'You knew the Tuckers? The family and the girl?'

'Oh, yes, of course, they've always been tenants on the estate. Mrs Tucker was the youngest of a large family. Her eldest brother was our head gardener. She married Alfred Tucker, who is a farm labourer—a stupid man but very nice. Mrs Tucker is a bit of a shrew. A good housewife, you know, and very clean in the house, but Tucker is never allowed to come anywhere farther than the scullery with his muddy boots on. All that sort of thing. She nags the children rather. Most of them have married and gone into jobs now. There was just this poor child, Marlene, left and three younger children. Two boys and a girl still at school.'

'Now, knowing the family as you do, Mrs Folliat, can you think of any reason why Marlene should have been killed today?'

'No, indeed I can't. It's quite, quite unbelievable, if you know what I mean, Inspector. There was no boyfriend or anything of that kind, or I shouldn't think so. Not that I've ever heard of, anyway.'

'Now what about the people who've been taking part in this Murder Hunt? Can you tell me anything about them?'

'Well, Mrs Oliver I'd never met before. She is quite unlike my idea of what a crime novelist would be. She's very upset, poor dear, by what has happened—naturally.'

'And what about the other helpers—Captain Warburton, for instance?'

'I don't see any reason why he should murder Marlene Tucker, if that's what you're asking me,' said Mrs Folliat composedly. 'I don't like him very much. He's what I call a foxy sort of man, but I suppose one has to be up to all the political tricks and all that kind of thing, if one is a political agent. He's certainly energetic and has worked very hard over this fête. I don't think he *could* have killed the girl, anyway, because he was on the lawn the whole time this afternoon.'

The inspector nodded.

'And the Legges? What do you know about the Legges?'

'Well, they seem a very nice young couple. He's inclined

to be what I should call—moody. I don't know very much about him. She was a Carstairs before her marriage and I know some relations of hers very well. They took the Mill Cottage for two months, and I hope they've enjoyed their holiday here. We've all got very friendly together.'

'She's an attractive lady, I understand.'

'Oh, yes, very attractive.'

'Would you say that at any time Sir George had felt that attraction?'

Mrs Folliat looked rather astonished.

'Oh, no, I'm sure there was nothing of that kind. Sir George is really absorbed by his business, and very fond of his wife. He's not at all a philandering sort of man.'

'And there was nothing, you would say, between Lady Stubbs and Mr Legge?'

Again Mrs Folliat shook her head.

'Oh, no, positively.'

The inspector persisted.

'There's been no trouble of any kind between Sir George and his wife, that you know of?'

'I'm sure there hasn't,' said Mrs Folliat, emphatically. 'And I would know if there had been.'

'It wouldn't be, then, as a result of any disagreement between husband and wife that Lady Stubbs has gone away?'

'Oh, no.' She added lightly, 'The silly girl, I understand, didn't want to meet this cousin of hers. Some childish phobia. So she's run away just like a child might do.'

'That's your opinion. Nothing more than that?'

'Oh, no. I expect she'll turn up again quite soon. Feeling rather ashamed of herself.' She added carelessly, 'What's become of this cousin, by the way? Is he still here in the house?'

'I understand he's gone back to his yacht.'

'And that's at Helmmouth, is it?'

'Yes, at Helmmouth.'

'I see,' said Mrs Folliat. 'Well, it's rather unfortunate— Hattie behaving so childishly. However, if he's staying on here for a day or so, we can make her see she must behave properly.'

It was, the inspector thought, a question, but although he noticed it he did not answer it.

'You are probably thinking,' he said, 'that all this is rather beside the point. But you do understand, don't you, Mrs Folliat, that we have to range over rather a wide field. Miss Brewis, for instance. What do you know about Miss Brewis?'

'Well, she's an excellent secretary. More than a secretary. She practically acts as housekeeper down here. In fact, I don't know what they'd do without her.'

'Was she Sir George's secretary before he married his wife?'

'I think so. I'm not quite sure. I've only known her since she came down here with them.'

'She doesn't like Lady Stubbs very much, does she?'

'No,' said Mrs Folliat, 'I'm afraid she doesn't. I don't think these good secretaries ever *do* care for wives much, if you know what I mean. Perhaps it's natural.'

'Was it you or Lady Stubbs who asked Miss Brewis to

take cakes and a fruit drink to the girl in the boat-house?'

Mrs Folliat looked slightly surprised.

'I remember Miss Brewis collecting some cakes and things and saying she was taking them along to Marlene. I didn't know anyone had particularly asked her to do it, or arranged about it. It certainly wasn't me.'

'I see. You say you were in the tea tent from four o'clock on. I believe Mrs Legge was also having tea in the tent at that time.'

'Mrs Legge? No, I don't think so. At least I don't remember seeing her there. In fact, I'm quite sure she wasn't there. We'd had a great influx by the bus from Torquay, and I remember looking round the tent and thinking that they must all be summer visitors; there was hardly a face there that I knew. I think Mrs Legge must have come in to tea later.'

'Oh, well,' said the inspector, 'it doesn't matter.' He added smoothly, 'Well, I really think that's all. Thank you, Mrs Folliat, you've been very kind. We can only hope that Lady Stubbs will return shortly.'

'I hope so, too,' said Mrs Folliat. 'Very thoughtless of the dear child giving us all so much anxiety.' She spoke briskly but the animation in her voice was not very natural. 'I'm sure,' said Mrs Folliat, 'that she's *quite* all right. Quite all right.'

At that moment the door opened and an attractive young woman with red hair and a freckled face came in, and said:

'I hear you've been asking for me?'

'This is Mrs Legge, Inspector,' said Mrs Folliat. 'Sally,

dear, I don't know whether you've heard about the terrible thing that has happened?'

'Oh, yes! Ghastly, isn't it?' said Mrs Legge. She uttered an exhausted sigh, and sank down in the chair as Mrs Folliat left the room.

'I'm terribly sorry about all this,' she said. 'It seems really unbelievable, if you know what I mean. I'm afraid I can't help you in any way. You see, I've been telling fortunes all the afternoon, so I haven't seen anything of what was going on.'

'I know, Mrs Legge. But we just have to ask everybody the same routine questions. For instance, just where were you between four-fifteen and five o'clock?'

'Well, I went and had tea at four o'clock.'

'In the tea tent?'

'Yes.'

'It was very crowded, I believe?'

'Oh, frightfully crowded.'

'Did you see anyone you knew there?'

'Oh, a few old people, yes. Nobody to speak to. Goodness, how I wanted that tea! That was four o'clock, as I say. I got back to the fortune-telling tent at half-past four and went on with my job. And goodness knows what I was promising the women in the end. Millionaire husbands, film stardom in Hollywood—heaven knows what. Mere journeys across the sea and suspicious dark women seemed too tame.'

'What happened during the half-hour when you were absent—I mean, supposing people wanted to have their fortunes told?'

'Oh, I hung a card up outside the tent. "Back at four-thirty."'

The inspector made a note in his pad.

'When did you last see Lady Stubbs?'

'Hattie? I don't really know. She was quite near at hand when I came out of the fortune-telling tent to go to tea, but I didn't speak to her. I don't remember seeing her afterwards. Somebody told me just now that she's missing. Is that true?'

'Yes, it is.'

'Oh, well,' said Sally Legge cheerfully, 'she's a bit queer in the top storey, you know. I dare say having a murder here has frightened her.'

'Well, thank you, Mrs Legge.'

Mrs Legge accepted the dismissal with promptitude. She went out, passing Hercule Poirot in the doorway.

III

Looking at the ceiling, the inspector spoke.

'Mrs Legge says she was in the tea tent between four and four-thirty. Mrs Folliat says she was helping in the tea tent from four o'clock on but that Mrs Legge was not among those present.' He paused and then went on, 'Miss Brewis says that Lady Stubbs asked her to take a tray of cakes and fruit juice to Marlene Tucker. Michael Weyman says that it's quite impossible Lady Stubbs should have done any such thing—it would be most uncharacteristic of her.'

'Ah,' said Poirot, 'the conflicting statements! Yes, one always has them.'

'And what a nuisance they are to clear up, too,' said the inspector. 'Sometimes they matter but in nine times out of ten they don't. Well, we've got to do a lot of spade work, that's clear.'

'And what do you think now, *mon cher*? What are the latest ideas?'

'I think,' said the inspector gravely, 'that Marlene Tucker saw something she was not meant to see. I think that it was because of what Marlene Tucker saw that she had to be killed.'

'I will not contradict you,' said Poirot. 'The point is what *did* she see?'

'She might have seen a murder,' said the inspector. 'Or she might have seen the person who did the murder.'

'Murder?' said Poirot. 'The murder of whom?'

'What do *you* think, Poirot? Is Lady Stubbs alive or dead?'

Poirot took a moment or two before he replied. Then he said:

'I think, *mon ami*, that Lady Stubbs is dead. And I will tell you *why* I think that. *It is because Mrs Folliat thinks she is dead.* Yes, whatever she may say now, or pretend to think, Mrs Folliat believes that Hattie Stubbs is dead. Mrs Folliat,' he added, 'knows a great deal that we do not.'

CHAPTER 12

Hercule Poirot came down to the breakfast table on the following morning to a depleted table. Mrs Oliver, still suffering from the shock of yesterday's occurrence, was having her breakfast in bed. Michael Weyman had had a cup of coffee and gone out early. Only Sir George and the faithful Miss Brewis were at the breakfast table. Sir George was giving indubitable proof of his mental condition by being unable to eat any breakfast. His plate lay almost untasted before him. He pushed aside the small pile of letters which, after opening them, Miss Brewis had placed before him. He drank coffee with an air of not knowing what he was doing. He said:

'Morning, M. Poirot,' perfunctorily, and then relapsed into his state of preoccupation. At times a few ejaculatory murmurs came from him.

'So incredible, the whole damn' thing. Where *can* she be?'

'The inquest will be held at the Institute on Thursday,' said Miss Brewis. 'They rang up to tell us.'

Agatha Christie

Her employer looked at her as if he did not understand.

'Inquest?' he said. 'Oh, yes, of course.' He sounded dazed and uninterested. After another sip or two of coffee he said, 'Women are incalculable. What does she think she's doing?'

Miss Brewis pursed her lips. Poirot observed acutely enough that she was in a state of taut nervous tension.

'Hodgson's coming to see you this morning,' she remarked, 'about the electrification of the milking sheds on the farm. And at twelve o'clock there's the—'

Sir George interrupted.

'I can't see anyone. Put 'em all off! How the devil d'you think a man can attend to business when he's worried half out of his mind about his wife?'

'If you say so, Sir George.' Miss Brewis gave the domestic equivalent of a barrister saying 'as your lordship pleases.' Her dissatisfaction was obvious.

'Never know,' said Sir George, 'what women get into their heads, or what fool things they're likely to do! You agree, eh?' he shot the last question at Poirot.

'*Les femmes?* They are incalculable,' said Poirot, raising his eyebrows and his hands with Gallic fervour. Miss Brewis blew her nose in an annoyed fashion.

'She *seemed* all right,' said Sir George. 'Damn' pleased about her new ring, dressed herself up to enjoy the fête. All just the same as usual. Not as though we'd had words or a quarrel of any kind. Going off without a word.'

'About those letters, Sir George,' began Miss Brewis.

'Damn the bloody letters to hell,' said Sir George, and pushed aside his coffee-cup.

146

He picked up the letters by his plate and more or less threw them at her.

'Answer them any way you like! I can't be bothered.' He went on more or less to himself, in an injured tone, 'Doesn't seem to be anything I can *do*... Don't even know if that police chap's any good. Very soft spoken and all that.'

'The police are, I believe,' said Miss Brewis, 'very efficient. They have ample facilities for tracing the whereabouts of missing persons.'

'They take days sometimes,' said Sir George, 'to find some miserable kid who's run off and hidden himself in a haystack.'

'I don't think Lady Stubbs is likely to be in a haystack, Sir George.'

'If only I could *do* something,' repeated the unhappy husband. 'I think, you know, I'll put an advertisement in the papers. Take it down, Amanda, will you?' He paused a moment in thought. '*Hattie. Please come home. Desperate about you. George.* All the papers, Amanda.'

Miss Brewis said acidly:

'Lady Stubbs doesn't often read the papers, Sir George. She's no interest at all in current affairs or what's going on in the world.' She added, rather cattily, but Sir George was not in the mood to appreciate cattiness, 'Of course you could put an advertisement in *Vogue*. That might catch her eye.'

Sir George said simply:

'Anywhere you think but get on with it.'

He got up and walked towards the door. With his hand

on the handle he paused and came back a few steps. He
spoke directly to Poirot.

'Look here, Poirot,' he said, '*you* don't think she's dead,
do you?'

Poirot fixed his eyes on his coffee-cup as he replied:

'I should say it is far too soon, Sir George, to assume
anything of that kind. There is no reason as yet to entertain
such an idea.'

'So you do think so,' said Sir George, heavily. 'Well,'
he added defiantly, 'I don't! *I* say she's quite all right.' He
nodded his head several times with increasing defiance, and
went out banging the door behind him.

Poirot buttered a piece of toast thoughtfully. In cases
where there was any suspicion of a wife being murdered,
he always automatically suspected the husband. (Similarly,
with a husband's demise, he suspected the wife.) But in
this case he did not suspect Sir George of having done
away with Lady Stubbs. From his brief observation of
them he was quite convinced that Sir George was devoted
to his wife. Moreover, as far as his excellent memory
served him (and it served him pretty well), Sir George had
been present on the lawn the entire afternoon until he
himself had left with Mrs Oliver to discover the body. He
had been there on the lawn when they had returned with
the news. No, it was not Sir George who was responsible
for Hattie's death. That is, if Hattie were dead. After all,
Poirot told himself, there was no reason to believe so as
yet. What he had just said to Sir George was true enough.
But in his own mind the conviction was unalterable. The

pattern, he thought, was the pattern of murder—a double murder.

Miss Brewis interrupted his thoughts by speaking with almost tearful venom.

'Men are such fools,' she said, 'such absolute *fools*! They're quite shrewd in most ways, and then they go marrying entirely the wrong sort of woman.'

Poirot was always willing to let people talk. The more people who talked to him, and the more they said, the better. There was nearly always a grain of wheat among the chaff.

'You think it has been an unfortunate marriage?' he demanded.

'Disastrous—quite disastrous.'

'You mean—that they were not happy together?'

'She'd a thoroughly bad influence over him in every way.'

'Now I find that very interesting. What kind of a bad influence?'

'Making him run to and fro at her beck and call, getting expensive presents out of him—far more jewels than one woman could wear. And furs. She's got two mink coats and a Russian ermine. What could any woman want with two mink coats, I'd like to know?'

Poirot shook his head.

'That I would not know,' he said.

'Sly,' continued Miss Brewis. 'Deceitful! Always playing the simpleton—especially when people were here. I suppose because she thought he liked her that way!'

'And did he like her that way?'

'Oh, men!' said Miss Brewis, her voice trembling on the

edge of hysteria. 'They don't appreciate efficiency or unselfishness, or loyalty or *any* one of those qualities! Now with a clever, capable wife Sir George would have got somewhere.'

'Got where?' asked Poirot.

'Well, he could take a prominent part in local affairs. Or stand for Parliament. He's a much more able man than poor Mr Masterton. I don't know if you've ever heard Mr Masterton on a platform—a most halting and uninspired speaker. He owes his position entirely to his wife. It's Mrs Masterton who's the power behind the throne. She's got all the drive and the initiative and the political acumen.'

Poirot shuddered inwardly at the thought of being married to Mrs Masterton, but he agreed quite truthfully with Miss Brewis' words.

'Yes,' he said, 'she is all that you say. A *femme formidable*,' he murmured to himself.

'Sir George doesn't seem ambitious,' went on Miss Brewis; 'he seems quite content to live here and potter about and play the country squire, and just go to London occasionally to attend to all his city directorships and all that, but he could make far more of himself than that with *his* abilities. He's really a very remarkable man, M. Poirot. That woman never understood him. She just regards him as a kind of machine for tipping out fur coats and jewels and expensive clothes. If he were married to someone who really appreciated his abilities...' She broke off, her voice wavering uncertainly.

Poirot looked at her with a real compassion. Miss Brewis was in love with her employer. She gave him a faithful, loyal and passionate devotion of which he was probably quite unaware and in which he would certainly not be interested. To Sir George, Amanda Brewis was an efficient machine who took the drudgery of daily life off his shoulders, who answered telephone calls, wrote letters, engaged servants, ordered meals and generally made life smooth for him. Poirot doubted if he had ever once thought of her as a woman. And that, he reflected, had its dangers. Women could work themselves up, they could reach an alarming pitch of hysteria unnoticed by the oblivious male who was the object of their devotion.

'A sly, scheming, clever cat, that's what she is,' said Miss Brewis tearfully.

'You say *is*, not *was*, I observe,' said Poirot.

'Of course she isn't dead!' said Miss Brewis, scornfully. 'Gone off with a man, that's what *she's* done! That's her type.'

'It is possible. It is always possible,' said Poirot. He took another piece of toast, inspected the marmalade pot gloomily and looked down the table to see if there were any kind of jam. There was none, so he resigned himself to butter.

'It's the only explanation,' said Miss Brewis. 'Of course *he* wouldn't think of it.'

'Has there—been any—trouble with men?' asked Poirot, delicately.

'Oh, she's been very clever,' said Miss Brewis.

'You mean you have not observed anything of the kind?'

'She'd be careful that I shouldn't,' said Miss Brewis.

151

'But you think that there may have been—what shall I say?—surreptitious episodes?'

'She's done her best to make a fool of Michael Weyman,' said Miss Brewis. 'Taking him down to see the camellia gardens at this time of year! Pretending she's so interested in the tennis pavilion.'

'After all, that is his business for being here and I understand Sir George is having it built principally to please his wife.'

'She's no good at tennis,' said Miss Brewis. 'She's no good at *any* games. Just wants an attractive setting to sit in, while other people run about and get hot. Oh, yes, she's done her best to make a fool of Michael Weyman. She'd probably have done it too, if he hadn't had other fish to fry.'

'Ah,' said Poirot, helping himself to a very little marmalade, placing it on the corner of a piece of toast and taking a mouthful dubiously. 'So he has other fish to fry, M. Weyman?'

'It was Mrs Legge who recommended him to Sir George,' said Miss Brewis. 'She knew him before she was married. Chelsea, I understand, and all that. She used to paint, you know.'

'She seems a very attractive and intelligent young woman,' said Poirot tentatively.

'Oh, yes, she's very intelligent,' said Miss Brewis. 'She's had a university education and I dare say could have made a career for herself if she hadn't married.'

'Has she been married long?'

'About three years, I believe. I don't think the marriage has turned out very well.'

'There is—incompatibility?'

'He's a queer young man, very moody. Wanders off a lot by himself and I've heard him very bad-tempered with her sometimes.'

'Ah, well,' said Poirot, 'the quarrels, the reconciliations, they are a part of early married life. Without them it is possible that life would be drab.'

'She's spent a good deal of time with Michael Weyman since he's been down here,' said Miss Brewis. 'I think he was in love with her before she married Alec Legge. I dare say it's only a flirtation on her side.'

'But Mr Legge was not pleased about it, perhaps?'

'One never knows with him, he's so vague. But I think he's been even moodier than usual, lately.'

'Did he admire Lady Stubbs, perhaps?'

'I dare say she thought he did. She thinks she only has to hold up a finger for any man to fall in love with her!'

'In any case, if she has gone off with a man, as you suggest, it is not Mr Weyman, for Mr Weyman is still here.'

'It's somebody she's been meeting on the sly, I've no doubt,' said Miss Brewis. 'She often slips out of the house on the quiet and goes off into the woods by herself. She was out the night before last. Yawning and saying she was going up to bed. I caught sight of her not half an hour later slipping out by the side door with a shawl over her head.'

Poirot looked thoughtfully at the woman opposite him.

He wondered if any reliance at all was to be placed in Miss Brewis' statements where Lady Stubbs was concerned, or whether it was entirely wishful thinking on her part. Mrs Folliat, he was sure, did not share Miss Brewis' ideas and Mrs Folliat knew Hattie much better than Miss Brewis could do. If Lady Stubbs had run away with a lover it would clearly suit Miss Brewis' book very well. She would be left to console the bereaved husband and to arrange for him efficiently the details of divorce. But that did not make it true, or probable, or even likely. If Hattie Stubbs had left with a lover, she had chosen a very curious time to do so, Poirot thought. For his own part he did not believe she had.

Miss Brewis sniffed through her nose and gathered together various scattered correspondence.

'If Sir George really wants those advertisements put in, I suppose I'd better see about it,' she said. 'Complete nonsense and waste of time. Oh, good morning, Mrs Masterton,' she added, as the door opened with authority and Mrs Masterton walked in.

'Inquest is set for Thursday, I hear,' she boomed. ' 'Morning, M. Poirot.'

Miss Brewis paused, her hand full of letters.

'Anything I can do for you, Mrs Masterton?' she asked.

'No, thank you, Miss Brewis. I expect you've plenty on your hands this morning, but I do want to thank you for all the excellent work you put in yesterday. You're such a good organizer and such a hard worker. We're all very grateful.'

'Thank you, Mrs Masterton.'

'Now don't let me keep you. I'll sit down and have a word with M. Poirot.'

'Enchanted, Madame,' said Poirot. He had risen to his feet and he bowed.

Mrs Masterton pulled out a chair and sat down. Miss Brewis left the room, quite restored to her usual efficient self.

'Marvellous woman, that,' said Mrs Masterton. 'Don't know what the Stubbses would do without her. Running a house takes some doing nowadays. Poor Hattie couldn't have coped with it. Extraordinary business, this, M. Poirot. I came to ask you what you thought about it.'

'What do you yourself think, Madame?'

'Well, it's an unpleasant thing to face, but I should say we've got some pathological character in this part of the world. Not a native, I hope. Perhaps been let out of an asylum—they're always letting 'em out half-cured nowadays. What I mean is, no one would ever want to strangle that Tucker girl. There couldn't be any motive, I mean, except some abnormal one. And if this man, whoever he is, *is* abnormal I should say he's probably strangled that poor girl, Hattie Stubbs, as well. She hasn't very much sense you know, poor child. If she met an ordinary-looking man and he asked her to come and look at something in the woods she'd probably go like a lamb, quite unsuspecting and docile.'

'You think her body is somewhere on the estate?'

'Yes, M. Poirot, I do. They'll find it once they search

155

around. Mind you, with about sixty-five acres of woodland here, it'll take some finding, if it's been dragged into the bushes or tumbled down a slope into the trees. What they need is bloodhounds,' said Mrs Masterton, looking, as she spoke, exactly like a bloodhound herself. 'Bloodhounds! I shall ring up the Chief Constable myself and say so.'

'It is very possible that you are right, Madame,' said Poirot. It was clearly the only thing one could say to Mrs Masterton.

'Of course I'm right,' said Mrs Masterton; 'but I must say, you know, it makes me very uneasy because the fellow is somewhere about. I'm calling in at the village when I leave here, telling the mothers to be very careful about their daughters—not let 'em go about alone. It's not a nice thought, M. Poirot, to have a killer in our midst.'

'A little point, Madame. How could a strange man have obtained admission to the boathouse? That would need a key.'

'Oh, that,' said Mrs Masterton, 'that's easy enough. She came out, of course.'

'Came out of the boathouse?'

'Yes. I expect she got bored, like girls do. Probably wandered out and looked about her. The most likely thing, I think, is that she actually saw Hattie Stubbs murdered. Heard a struggle or something, went to see and the man, having disposed of Lady Stubbs, naturally had to kill her too. Easy enough for him to take her back to the boathouse, dump her there and come out, pulling the door behind him. It was a Yale lock. It would pull to, and lock.'

Poirot nodded gently. It was not his purpose to argue with Mrs Masterton or to point out to her the interesting fact which she had completely overlooked, that if Marlene Tucker had been killed away from the boathouse, somebody must have known enough about the murder game to put her back in the exact place and position which the victim was supposed to assume. Instead, he said gently:

'Sir George Stubbs is confident that his wife is still alive.'

'That's what he says, man, because he wants to believe it. He was very devoted to her, you know.' She added, rather unexpectedly, 'I like George Stubbs in spite of his origins and his city background and all that, he goes down very well in the county. The worst that can be said about him is that he's a bit of a snob. And after all, social snobbery's harmless enough.'

Poirot said somewhat cynically:

'In these days, Madame, surely money has become as acceptable as good birth.'

'My dear man, I couldn't agree with you more. There's no need for him to be a snob—only got to buy the place and throw his money about, and we'd all come and call! But actually, the man's liked. It's not only his money. Of course Amy Folliat's had something to do with that. She has sponsored them, and mind you, she's got a lot of influence in this part of the world. Why, there have been Folliats here since Tudor times.'

'There have always been Folliats at Nasse House,' Poirot murmured to himself.

'Yes.' Mrs Masterton sighed. 'It's sad, the toll taken by

the war. Young men killed in battle—death duties and all that. Then whoever comes into a place can't afford to keep it up and has to sell—'

'But Mrs Folliat, although she has lost her home, still lives on the estate.'

'Yes. She's made the Lodge quite charming too. Have you been inside it?'

'No, we parted at the door.'

'It wouldn't be everybody's cup of tea,' said Mrs Masterton. 'To live at the lodge of your old home and see strangers in possession. But to do Amy Folliat justice I don't think she feels bitter about that. In fact, she engineered the whole thing. There's no doubt she imbued Hattie with the idea of living down here, and got her to persuade George Stubbs into it. The thing, I think, that Amy Folliat couldn't have borne was to see the place turned into a hostel or institution, or carved up for building.' She rose to her feet. 'Well, I must be getting along. I'm a busy woman.'

'Of course. You have to talk to the Chief Constable about bloodhounds.'

Mrs Masterton gave a sudden deep bay of laughter. 'Used to breed 'em at one time,' she said. 'People tell me I'm a bit like a bloodhound myself.'

Poirot was slightly taken aback and she was quick enough to see it.

'I bet you've been thinking so, M. Poirot,' she said.

CHAPTER 13

After Mrs Masterton had left, Poirot went out and strolled through the woods. His nerves were not quite what they should be. He felt an irresistible desire to look behind every bush and to consider every thicket of rhododendron as a possible hiding-place for a body. He came at last to the Folly and, going inside it, he sat down on the stone bench there, to rest his feet which were, as was his custom, enclosed in tight, pointed patent-leather shoes.

Through the trees he could catch faint glimmers of the river and of the wooded banks on the opposite side. He found himself agreeing with the young architect that this was no place to put an architectural fantasy of this kind. Gaps could be cut in the trees, of course, but even then there would be no proper view. Whereas, as Michael Weyman had said, on the grassy bank near the house a Folly could have been erected with a delightful vista right down the river to Helmmouth. Poirot's thoughts flew off at a tangent. Helmmouth, the yacht *Espérance*, and Etienne de Sousa.

159

The whole thing must tie up in some kind of pattern, but what the pattern was he could not visualize. Tempting strands of it showed here and there but that was all.

Something that glittered caught his eye and he bent to pick it up. It had come to rest in a small crack of the concrete base to the temple. He held it in the palm of his hand and looked at it with a faint stirring of recognition. It was a little gold aeroplane charm. As he frowned at it, a picture came into his mind. A bracelet. A gold bracelet hung over with dangling charms. He was sitting once more in the tent and the voice of Madame Zuleika, alias Sally Legge, was talking of dark women and journeys across the sea and good fortune in a letter. Yes, she had had on a bracelet from which depended a multiplicity of small gold objects. One of these modern fashions which repeated the fashions of Poirot's early days. Probably that was why it had made an impression on him. Some time or other, presumably, Mrs Legge had sat here in the Folly, and one of the charms had fallen from her bracelet. Perhaps she had not even noticed it. It might have been yesterday afternoon...

Poirot considered that latter point. Then he heard footsteps outside and looked up sharply. A figure came round to the front of the Folly and stopped, startled, at the sight of Poirot. Poirot looked with a considering eye on the slim, fair young man wearing a shirt on which a variety of tortoise and turtle was depicted. The shirt was unmistakable. He had observed it closely yesterday when its wearer was throwing coconuts.

He noticed that the young man was almost unusually perturbed. He said quickly in a foreign accent:

'I beg your pardon—I did not know—'

Poirot smiled gently at him but with a reproving air.

'I am afraid,' he said, 'that you are trespassing.'

'Yes, I am sorry.'

'You come from the hostel?'

'Yes. Yes, I do. I thought perhaps one could get through the woods this way and so to the quay.'

'I am afraid,' said Poirot gently, 'that you will have to go back the way you came. There is no through road.'

The young man said again, showing all his teeth in a would-be agreeable smile:

'I am sorry. I am very sorry.'

He bowed and turned away.

Poirot came out of the Folly and back on to the path, watching the boy retreat. When he got to the ending of the path, he looked over his shoulder. Then, seeing Poirot watching him, he quickened his pace and disappeared round the bend.

'*Eh bien,*' said Poirot to himself, 'is this a murderer I have seen, or is it not?'

The young man had certainly been at the fête yesterday and had scowled when he had collided with Poirot, and just as certainly therefore he must know quite well that there was no through path by way of the woods to the ferry. If, indeed, he *had* been looking for a path to the ferry he would not have taken this path by the Folly, but would have kept on the lower level near the river. Moreover, he

161

had arrived at the Folly with the air of one who has reached his rendezvous, and who is badly startled at finding the wrong person at the meeting place.

'So it is like this,' said Poirot to himself. 'He came here to meet someone. Who did he come to meet?' He added as an afterthought, 'And why?'

He strolled down to the bend of the path and looked at it where it wound away into the trees. There was no sign of the young man in the turtle shirt now. Presumably he had deemed it prudent to retreat as rapidly as possible. Poirot retraced his steps, shaking his head.

Lost in thought, he came quietly round the side of the Folly, and stopped on the threshold, startled in his turn. Sally Legge was there on her knees, her head bent down to the cracks in the flooring. She jumped up, startled.

'Oh, M. Poirot, you gave me such a shock. I didn't hear you coming.'

'You were looking for something, Madame?'

'I—no, not exactly.'

'You had lost something, perhaps,' said Poirot. 'Dropped something. Or perhaps...' He adopted a roguish, gallant air, 'Or perhaps, Madame, it is a rendezvous. I am, most unfortunately, not the person you came to meet?'

She had recovered her aplomb by now.

'Does one ever have rendezvous in the middle of the morning?' she demanded, questioningly.

'Sometimes,' said Poirot, 'one has to have a rendezvous at the only time one can. Husbands,' he added sententiously, 'are sometimes jealous.'

'I doubt if mine is,' said Sally Legge.

She said the words lightly enough, but behind them Poirot heard an undertone of bitterness.

'He's so completely engrossed in his own affairs.'

'All women complain of that in husbands,' said Poirot. 'Especially in English husbands,' he added.

'You foreigners are more gallant.'

'We know,' said Poirot, 'that it is necessary to tell a woman at least once a week, and preferably three or four times, that we love her; and that it is also wise to bring her a few flowers, to pay her a few compliments, to tell her that she looks well in her new dress or new hat.'

'Is that what *you* do?'

'I, Madame, am not a husband,' said Hercule Poirot. 'Alas!' he added.

'I'm sure there's no alas about it. I'm sure you're quite delighted to be a carefree bachelor.'

'No, no, Madame, it is terrible all that I have missed in life.'

'I think one's a fool to marry,' said Sally Legge.

'You regret the days when you painted in your studio in Chelsea?'

'You seem to know all about me, M. Poirot?'

'I am a gossip,' said Hercule Poirot. 'I like to hear all about people.' He went on, 'Do you really regret, Madame?'

'Oh, I don't know.' She sat down impatiently on the seat. Poirot sat beside her.

He witnessed once more the phenomenon to which he was becoming accustomed. This attractive, redhaired girl was about to say things to him that she would have thought twice about saying to an Englishman.

'I hoped,' she said, 'that when we came down here for a holiday away from everything, that things would be the same again... But it hasn't worked out like that.'

'No?'

'No. Alec's just as moody and—oh, I don't know—wrapped up in himself. I don't know what's the matter with him. He's so nervy and on edge. People ring him up and leave queer messages for him and he won't tell me *anything*. That's what makes me mad. He won't *tell* me anything! I thought at first it was some other woman, but I don't think it is. Not really...'

But her voice held a certain doubt which Poirot was quick to notice.

'Did you enjoy your tea yesterday afternoon, Madame?' he asked.

'Enjoy my tea?' She frowned at him, her thoughts seeming to come back from a long way away. Then she said hastily, 'Oh, yes. You've no idea how exhausting it was, sitting in that tent muffled up in all those veils. It was stifling.'

'The tea tent also must have been somewhat stifling?'

'Oh, yes, it was. However, there's nothing like a cuppa, is there?'

'You were searching for something just now, were you not, Madame? Would it, by any possibility, be this?' He held out in his hand the little gold charm.

'I—oh, yes. Oh, thank you, M. Poirot. Where did you find it?'

'It was here, on the floor, in that crack over there.'

'I must have dropped it some time.'

'Yesterday?'

'Oh, no, not yesterday. It was before that.'

'But surely, Madame, I remember seeing that particular charm on your wrist when you were telling me my fortune.'

Nobody could tell a deliberate lie better than Hercule Poirot. He spoke with complete assurance and before that assurance Sally Legge's eyelids dropped.

'I don't really remember,' she said. 'I only noticed this morning that it was missing.'

'Then I am happy,' said Poirot gallantly, 'to be able to restore it to you.'

She was turning the little charm over nervously in her fingers. Now she rose.

'Well, thank you, M. Poirot, thank you very much,' she said. Her breath was coming rather unevenly and her eyes were nervous.

She hurried out of the Folly. Poirot leaned back in the seat and nodded his head slowly.

No, he said to himself, no, you did not go to the tea tent yesterday afternoon. It was not because you wanted your tea that you were so anxious to know if it was four o'clock. It was *here* you came yesterday afternoon. Here, to the Folly. *Halfway to the boathouse.* You came here to meet someone.

Once again he heard footsteps approaching. Rapid impatient footsteps. 'And here perhaps,' said Poirot, smiling in anticipation, 'comes whoever it was that Mrs Legge came up here to meet.'

But then, as Alec Legge came round the corner of the Folly, Poirot ejaculated:

'Wrong again.'

'Eh? What's that?' Alec Legge looked startled.

'I said,' explained Poirot, 'that I was wrong again. I am not often wrong,' he explained, 'and it exasperates me. It was not you I expected to see.'

'Whom did you expect to see?' asked Alec Legge.

Poirot replied promptly.

'A young man—a boy almost—in one of these gaily-patterned shirts with turtles on it.'

He was pleased at the effect of his words. Alec Legge took a step forward. He said rather incoherently:

'How do you know? How did—what d'you mean?'

'I am psychic,' said Hercule Poirot, and closed his eyes.

Alec Legge took another couple of steps forward. Poirot was conscious that a very angry man was standing in front of him.

'What the devil did you mean?' he demanded.

'Your friend has, I think,' said Poirot, 'gone back to the Youth Hostel. If you want to see him you will have to go there to find him.'

'So that's it,' muttered Alec Legge.

He dropped down at the other end of the stone bench.

'So that's why you're down here? It wasn't a question of "giving away the prizes." I might have known better.' He turned towards Poirot. His face was haggard and unhappy. 'I know what it must seem like,' he said. 'I know what the whole thing looks like. But it isn't as you think it is. I'm being victimized. I tell you that once you get into these people's clutches, it isn't so easy to get out of them. And I want to get out of them. That's the point. *I want to get out of them.* You get desperate, you know. You feel like taking desperate measures. You feel you're caught like a rat in a trap and there's nothing you can do. Oh, well, what's the good of talking! You know what you want to know now, I suppose. You've got your evidence.'

He got up, stumbled a little as though he could hardly see his way, then rushed off energetically without a backward look.

Hercule Poirot remained behind with his eyes very wide open and his eyebrows rising.

'All this is very curious,' he murmured. 'Curious and interesting. I have the evidence I need, have I? Evidence of what? Murder?'

CHAPTER 14

Inspector Bland sat in Helmmouth Police Station. Superintendent Baldwin, a large comfortable-looking man, sat on the other side of the table. Between the two men, on the table, was a black sodden mass. Inspector Bland poked at it with a cautious forefinger.

'That's her hat all right,' he said. 'I'm sure of it, though I don't suppose I could swear to it. She fancied that shape, it seems. So her maid told me. She'd got one or two of them. A pale pink and a sort of puce colour, but yesterday she was wearing the black one. Yes, this is it. And you fished it out of the river? That makes it look as though it's the way we think it is.'

'No certainty yet,' said Baldwin. 'After all,' he added, 'anyone could throw a hat into the river.'

'Yes,' said Bland, 'they could throw it in from the boat-house, or they could throw it in off a yacht.'

'The yacht's sewed up, all right,' said Baldwin. 'If she's there, alive or dead, she's still there.'

'He hasn't been ashore today?'

'Not so far. He's on board. He's been sitting out in a deck-chair smoking a cigar.'

Inspector Bland glanced at the clock.

'Almost time to go aboard,' he said.

'Think you'll find her?' asked Baldwin.

'I wouldn't bank on it,' said Bland. 'I've got the feeling, you know, that he's a clever devil.' He was lost in thought for a moment, poking again at the hat. Then he said, 'What about the body—if there was a body? Any ideas about that?'

'Yes,' said Baldwin, 'I talked to Otterweight this morning. Ex-coastguard man. I always consult him in anything to do with tides and currents. About the time the lady went into the Helm, if she did go into the Helm, the tide was just on the ebb. There is a full moon now and it would be flowing swiftly. Reckon she'd be carried out to sea and the current would take her towards the Cornish coast. There's no certainty where the body would fetch up or if it would fetch up at all. One or two drownings we've had here, we've never recovered the body. It gets broken up, too, on the rocks. Here, by Start Point. On the other hand, it *might* fetch up any day.'

'If it doesn't, it's going to be difficult,' said Bland.

'You're certain in your own mind that she did go into the river?'

'I don't see what else it can be,' said Inspector Bland sombrely. 'We've checked up, you know, on the buses and the trains. This place is a cul-de-sac. She was wearing conspicuous clothes and she didn't take any others with her. So I should say she never left Nasse. Either her body's in the sea or else it's hidden somewhere on the property. What I want now,' he went on heavily, 'is *motive*. And the body of course,' he added, as an afterthought. 'Can't get anywhere until I find the body.'

'What about the other girl?'

'She saw it—or she saw something. We'll get at the facts in the end, but it won't be easy.'

Baldwin in his turn looked up at the clock.

'Time to go,' he said.

The two police officers were received on board the *Espérance* with all De Sousa's charming courtesy. He offered them drinks which they refused, and went on to express a kindly interest in their activities.

'You are farther forward with your inquiries regarding the death of this young girl?'

'We're progressing,' Inspector Bland told him.

The superintendent took up the running and expressed very delicately the object of their visit.

'You would like to search the *Espérance*?' De Sousa did not seem annoyed. Instead he seemed rather amused. 'But why? You think I conceal the murderer or do you think perhaps that I am the murderer myself?'

'It's necessary, Mr De Sousa, as I'm sure you'll understand. A search warrant...'

De Sousa raised his hands.

'But I am anxious to co-operate—eager! Let this be all among friends. You are welcome to search where you will in my boat. Ah, perhaps you think that I have here my cousin, Lady Stubbs? You think, perhaps, she has run away from her husband and taken shelter with me? But search, gentlemen, by all means search.'

The search was duly undertaken. It was a thorough one. In the end, striving to conceal their chagrin, the two police officers took leave of Mr De Sousa.

'You have found nothing? How disappointing. But I told you that was so. You will perhaps have some refreshment now. No?'

He accompanied them to where their boat lay alongside.

'And for myself?' he asked. 'I am free to depart? You understand it becomes a little boring here. The weather is good. I should like very much to proceed to Plymouth.'

'If you would be kind enough, sir, to remain here for the inquest—that is tomorrow—in case the Coroner should wish to ask you anything.'

'Why, certainly. I want to do all that I can. But after that?'

'After that, sir,' said Superintendent Baldwin, his face wooden, 'you are, of course, at liberty to proceed where you will.'

The last thing they saw as the launch moved away from the yacht was De Sousa's smiling face looking down on them.

II

The inquest was almost painfully devoid of interest. Apart from the medical evidence and evidence of identity, there was little to feed the curiosity of the spectators. An adjournment was asked for and granted. The whole proceedings had been purely formal.

What followed the inquest, however, was not quite so formal. Inspector Bland spent the afternoon taking a trip in that well-known pleasure steamer, the *Devon Belle*. Leaving Brixwell at about three o'clock, it rounded the headland, proceeded around the coast, entered the mouth of the Helm and went up the river. There were about two hundred and thirty people on board besides Inspector Bland. He sat on the starboard side of the boat, scanning the wooded shore. They came round a bend in the river and passed the isolated grey tiled boathouse that belonged to Hoodown Park. Inspector Bland looked surreptitiously at his watch. It was just quarter-past four. They were coming now close beside the Nasse boathouse. It nestled remote in its trees with its little balcony and its small quay below. There was no sign apparent that there was anyone inside the boathouse, though as a matter of fact, to Inspector Bland's certain knowledge, there *was* someone inside. P.C. Hoskins, in accordance with orders, was on duty there.

Not far from the boathouse steps was a small launch. In the launch were a man and girl in holiday kit. They were indulging in what seemed like some rather rough horseplay. The girl was screaming, the man was playfully pretending he was going to duck her overboard. At that same moment a stentorian voice spoke through a megaphone.

'Ladies and gentlemen,' it boomed, 'you are now approaching the famous village of Gitcham where we shall remain for three-quarters of an hour and where you can have a crab or lobster tea, as well as Devonshire cream. On your right are the grounds of Nasse House. You will pass the house itself in two or three minutes, it is just visible through the trees. Originally the home of Sir Gervase Folliat, a contemporary of Sir Francis Drake who sailed with him in his voyage to the new world, it is now the property of Sir George Stubbs. On your left is the famous Gooseacre Rock. There, ladies and gentlemen, it was the habit to deposit scolding wives at low tide and leave them there until the water came up to their necks.'

Everybody on the *Devon Belle* stared with fascinated interest at the Gooseacre Rock. Jokes were made and there were many shrill giggles and guffaws.

While this was happening, the holidaymaker in the boat, with a final scuffle, did push his lady friend overboard. Leaning over, he held her in the water, laughing and saying, 'No, I don't pull you out till you've promised to behave.'

Nobody, however, observed this with the exception of Inspector Bland. They had all been listening to the megaphone, staring for the first sight of Nasse House through the trees, and gazing with fascinated interest at the Gooseacre Rock.

The holidaymaker released the girl, she sank under water and a few moments later appeared on the other side of the boat. She swam to it and got in, heaving herself over the side with practised skill. Policewoman Alice Jones was an accomplished swimmer.

Inspector Bland came ashore at Gitcham with the other two hundred and thirty passengers and consumed a lobster tea with Devonshire cream and scones. He said to himself as he did so, 'So it *could* be done, and no one would notice!'

III

While Inspector Bland was doing his experiment on the Helm, Hercule Poirot was experimenting with a tent on the lawn at Nasse House. It was, in actual fact, the same tent where Madame Zuleika had told her fortunes. When the rest of the marquees and stands had been dismantled Poirot had asked for this to remain behind.

He went into it now, closed the flaps and went to the back of it. Deftly he unlaced the flaps there, slipped out, relaced them, and plunged into the hedge of rhododendron that immediately backed the tent. Slipping between a couple of bushes, he soon reached a small rustic arbour. It was a kind of summer-house with a closed door. Poirot opened the door and went inside.

It was very dim inside because very little light came in through the rhododendrons which had grown up round it since it had been first placed there many years ago. There was a box there with croquet balls in it, and some old rusted hoops. There were one or two broken hockey sticks, a good many earwigs and spiders, and a round irregular mark on the dust on the floor. At this Poirot looked for some time. He knelt down, and taking a little yard measure from his pocket, he measured its dimensions carefully. Then he nodded his head in a satisfied fashion.

He slipped out quietly, shutting the door behind him.

Then he pursued an oblique course through the rhododendron bushes. He worked his way up the hill in this way and came out a short time after on the path which led to the Folly and down from there to the boathouse.

He did not visit the Folly this time, but went straight down the zig-zagging way until he reached the boathouse. He had the key with him and he opened the door and went in.

Except for the removal of the body, and of the tea tray with its glass and plate, it was just as he remembered it. The police had noted and photographed all that it contained. He went over now to the table where the pile of comics lay. He turned them over and his expression was not unlike Inspector Bland's had been as he noted the words Marlene had doodled down there before she died. 'Jackie Blake goes with Susan Brown.' 'Peter pinches girls at the pictures.' 'Georgie Porgie kisses hikers in the wood.' 'Biddy Fox likes boys.' 'Albert goes with Doreen.'

He found the remarks pathetic in their young crudity. He remembered Marlene's plain, rather spotty face. He suspected that boys had not pinched Marlene at the pictures. Frustrated, Marlene had got a vicarious thrill by her spying and peering at her young contemporaries. She had spied on people, she had snooped, and she had seen things. Things that she was not meant to have seen—things, usually, of small importance, but on one occasion perhaps something of more importance? Something of whose importance she herself had had no idea.

It was all conjecture, and Poirot shook his head

doubtfully. He replaced the pile of comics neatly on the table, his passion for tidiness always in the ascendent. As he did so, he was suddenly assailed with the feeling of something missing. Something... What was it? Something that *ought* to have been there... Something... He shook his head as the elusive impression faded.

He went slowly out of the boathouse, unhappy and displeased with himself. He, Hercule Poirot, had been summoned to prevent a murder—and he had not prevented it. It had happened. What was even more humiliating was that he had no real ideas, even now, as to what had actually happened. It was ignominious. And tomorrow he must return to London defeated. His ego was seriously deflated—even his moustaches drooped.

CHAPTER 15

It was a fortnight later that Inspector Bland had a long and unsatisfying interview with the Chief Constable of the County.

Major Merrall had irritable tufted eyebrows and looked rather like an angry terrier. But his men all liked him and respected his judgment.

'Well, well, well,' said Major Merrall. 'What have we got? Nothing that we can act on. This fellow De Sousa now? We can't connect him in any way with the Girl Guide. If Lady Stubbs' body had turned up, that would have been different.' He brought his eyebrows down towards his nose and glared at Bland. 'You think there *is* a body, don't you?'

'What do you think, sir?'

'Oh, I agree with you. Otherwise, we'd have traced her by now. Unless, of course, she'd made her plans very carefully. And I don't see the least indication of that. She'd no money, you know. We've been into all the financial side of it. Sir George had the money. He made her a very generous allowance, but she's not got a stiver of her own. And there's no trace of a lover. No rumour of one, no gossip—and there would be, mark you, in a country district like that.'

He took a turn up and down the floor.

'The plain fact of it is that we don't know. We *think* De Sousa for some unknown reason of his own made away with his cousin. The most probable thing is that he got her to meet him down at the boathouse, took her aboard the launch and pushed her overboard. You've tested that that could happen?'

'Good lord, sir! You could drown a whole boatful of people during holiday time in the river or on the seashore. Nobody'd think anything of it. Everyone spends their time squealing and pushing each other off things. But the thing De Sousa *didn't* know about, was that that girl was in the boathouse, bored to death with nothing to do and ten to one was looking out of the window.'

'Hoskins looked out of the window and watched the performance you put up, and you didn't see him?'

'No, sir. You'd have no idea anyone was in that boat-house unless they came out on the balcony and showed themselves—'

'Perhaps the girl did come out on the balcony. De Sousa realizes she's seen what he's doing, so he comes ashore and deals with her, gets her to let him into the boathouse by asking her what she's doing there. She tells him, pleased with her part in the Murder Hunt, he puts the cord round her neck in a playful manner—and whooooosh...' Major Merrall made an expressive gesture with his hands. 'That's that! Okay, Bland; okay. Let's say that's how it happened. Pure guesswork. We haven't got *any* evidence. We haven't

178

got a body, and if we attempted to detain De Sousa in this country we'd have a hornets' nest about our ears. We'll have to let him go.'

'*Is* he going, sir?'

'He's laying up his yacht a week from now. Going back to his blasted island.'

'So we haven't got much time,' said Inspector Bland gloomily.

'There are other possibilities, I suppose?'

'Oh, yes, sir, there are several *possibilities*. I still hold to it that she must have been murdered by somebody who was in on the facts of the Murder Hunt. We can clear two people completely. Sir George Stubbs and Captain Warburton. They were running shows on the lawn and taking charge of things the entire afternoon. They are vouched for by dozens of people. The same applies to Mrs Masterton, if, that is, one can include her at all.'

'Include everybody,' said Major Merrall. 'She's continually ringing me up about bloodhounds. In a detective story,' he added wistfully, 'she'd be just the woman who *had* done it. But, dash it, I've known Connie Masterton pretty well all my life. I just can't see her going round strangling Girl Guides, or disposing of mysterious exotic beauties. Now, then, who else is there?'

'There's Mrs Oliver,' said Bland. 'She devised the Murder Hunt. She's rather eccentric and she was away on her own for a good part of the afternoon. Then there's Mr Alec Legge.'

'Fellow in the pink cottage, eh?'

'Yes. He left the show fairly early on, or he wasn't seen

there. He says he got fed up with it and walked back to his cottage. On the other hand, old Merdell—that's the old boy down at the quay who looks after people's boats for them and helps with the parking—he says Alec Legge passed him going back to the cottage about five o'clock. Not earlier. That leaves about an hour of his time unaccounted for. He says, of course, that Merdell has no idea of time and was quite wrong as to when he saw him. And after all, the old man *is* ninety-two.'

'Rather unsatisfactory,' said Major Merrall. 'No motive or anything of that kind to tie him in?'

'He might have been having an affair with Lady Stubbs,' said Bland doubtfully, 'and she might have been threatening to tell his wife, and he might have done her in, and the girl might have seen it happen—'

'And he concealed Lady Stubbs' body somewhere?'

'Yes. But I'm blessed if I know how or where. My men have searched that sixty-five acres and there's no trace anywhere of disturbed earth, and I should say that by now we've rooted under every bush there is. Still, say he did manage to hide the body, he could have thrown her hat into the river as a blind. And Marlene Tucker saw him and so he disposed of her? That part of it's always the same.' Inspector Bland paused, then said, 'And, of course, there's Mrs Legge—'

'What have we got on her?'

'She wasn't in the tea tent from four to half past as she says she was,' said Inspector Bland slowly. 'I spotted that as soon as I'd talked to her and to Mrs Folliat. Evidence supports Mrs Folliat's statement. And that's the particular, vital half-hour.'

Again he paused. 'Then there's the architect, young Michael Weyman. It's difficult to tie him up with it in any way, but he's what I should call a *likely* murderer—one of those cocky, nervy young fellows. Would kill anyone and not turn a hair about it. In with a loose set, I shouldn't wonder.'

'You're so damned respectable, Bland,' said Major Merrall. 'How does he account for his movements?'

'Very vague, sir. Very vague indeed.'

'That proves he's a genuine architect,' said Major Merrall with feeling. He had recently built himself a house near the sea coast. 'They're so vague, I wonder they're alive at all sometimes.'

'Doesn't know where he was or when and there's nobody who seems to have seen him. There *is* some evidence that Lady Stubbs was keen on him.'

'I suppose you're hinting at one of these sex murders?'

'I'm only looking about for what I can find, sir,' said Inspector Bland with dignity. 'And then there's Miss Brewis...' He paused. It was a long pause.

'That's the secretary, isn't it?'

'Yes, sir. Very efficient woman.'

Again there was a pause. Major Merrall eyed his subordinate keenly.

'You've got something on your mind about her, haven't you?' he said.

'Yes, I have, sir. You see, she admits quite openly that she was in the boathouse at about the time the murder must have been committed.'

'Would she do that if she was guilty?'

'She might,' said Inspector Bland slowly. 'Actually, it's the best thing she could do. You see, if she picks up a tray with cake and a fruit drink and tells everyone she's taking that for the child down there—well, then, her presence is accounted for. She goes there and comes back and says the girl was alive at that time. We've taken her word for it. But if you remember, sir, and look again at the medical evidence, Dr Cook's time of death is between four o'clock and quarter to five. We've only Miss Brewis' word for it that Marlene was alive at a quarter past four. And there's one curious point that came up about her testimony. She told me that it was Lady Stubbs who told her to take the cakes and fruit drink to Marlene. But another witness said quite definitely that that wasn't the sort of thing that Lady Stubbs would think about. And I think, you know, that they're right there. It's not like Lady Stubbs. Lady Stubbs was a dumb beauty wrapped up in herself and her own appearance. She never seems to have ordered meals or taken an interest in household management or thought of anybody at all except her own handsome self. The more I think of it, the more it seems most unlikely that she *should* have told Miss Brewis to take anything to the Girl Guide.'

'You know, Bland,' said Merrall, 'you've got something there. But what's her motive, if so?'

'No motive for killing the girl,' said Bland; 'but I do think, you know, that she might have a motive for killing Lady Stubbs. According to M. Poirot, whom I told you about, she's head over heels in love with her employer. Supposing she followed Lady Stubbs into the woods and killed her and that Marlene Tucker, bored in the boathouse, came out and happened to see it? Then of course she'd have to kill Marlene too. What would she do next? Put the girl's body in the boathouse, come back to the house, fetch the tray and go down to the boathouse again. Then she's covered her own absence from the fête and we've got *her* testimony, our only reliable testimony on the face of it, *that Marlene Tucker was alive at a quarter past four.*'

'Well,' said Major Merrall, with a sigh, 'keep after it, Bland. Keep after it. What do you think she did with Lady Stubbs' body, if she's the guilty party?'

'Hid it in the woods, buried it, or threw it into the river.'

'The last would be rather difficult, wouldn't it?'

'It depends where the murder was committed,' said the inspector. 'She's quite a hefty woman. If it was not far from the boathouse, she *could* have carried her down there and thrown her off the edge of the quay.'

'With every pleasure steamer on the Helm looking on?'

'It would be just another piece of horse-play. Risky, but possible. But I think it far more likely myself that she hid the body somewhere, and just threw the hat into the Helm. It's possible, you see, that she, knowing the house and grounds well, might know some place where you could conceal a body. She may have managed to dispose of it in the river later. Who knows? That is, of course, if she did it,' added Inspector Bland as an afterthought. 'But, actually, sir, I stick to De Sousa—'

Major Merrall had been noting down points on a pad. He looked up now, clearing his throat.

'It comes to this, then. We can summarize it as follows: we've got five or six people who *could* have killed Marlene Tucker. Some of them are more likely than others, but that's as far as we can go. In a general way, we know *why* she was killed. She was killed because she saw something. But until we know *exactly* what it was she saw—*we don't know who killed her.*'

'Put like that, you make it sound a bit difficult, sir.'

'Oh, it *is* difficult. But we shall get there—in the end.'

'And meantime that chap will have left England—laughing in his sleeve—having got away with two murders.'

'You're fairly sure about him, aren't you? I don't say you're wrong. All the same...'

The chief constable was silent for a moment or two, then he said, with a shrug of his shoulders:

'Anyway, it's better than having one of these psychopathic murderers. We'd probably be having a third murder on our hands by now.'

'They do say things go in threes,' said the inspector gloomily.

He repeated that remark the following morning when he heard that old Merdell, returning home from a visit to his favourite pub across the river at Gitcham, must have exceeded his usual potations and had fallen in the river when boarding the quay. His boat was found adrift, and the old man's body was recovered that evening.

The inquest was short and simple. The night had been dark and overcast, old Merdell had had three pints of beer and, after all, he was ninety-two.

The verdict brought in was Accidental Death.

CHAPTER 16

Hercule Poirot sat in a square chair in front of the square fireplace in the square room of his London flat. In front of him were various objects that were not square: that were instead violently and almost impossibly curved. Each of them, studied separately, looked as if it could not have any conceivable function in a sane world. They appeared improbable, irresponsible, and wholly fortuitous. In actual fact, of course, they were nothing of the sort.

Assessed correctly, each had its particular place in a particular universe. Assembled in their proper place in their particular universe, they not only made sense, they made a picture. In other words, Hercule Poirot was doing a jigsaw puzzle.

He looked down at where a rectangle still showed improbably shaped gaps. It was an occupation he found soothing and pleasant. It brought disorder into order. It had, he reflected, a certain resemblance to his own profession. There, too, one was faced with various improbably shaped and unlikely facts which, though seeming to bear no relationship to each other, yet did each have its properly balanced part in assembling the whole. His fingers deftly picked up an improbable piece of dark grey and fitted it into a blue sky. It was, he now perceived, part of an aeroplane.

'Yes,' murmured Poirot to himself, 'that is what one must do. The unlikely piece here, the improbable piece there, the oh-so-rational piece that is not what it seems; all of these have their appointed place, and once they are fitted in, *eh bien*, there is an end of the business! All is clear. All is—as they say nowadays—*in the picture*.'

He fitted in, in rapid succession, a small piece of a minaret, another piece that looked as though it was part of a striped awning and was actually the backside of a cat, and a missing piece of sunset that had changed with Turneresque sudden-ness from orange to pink.

If one knew what to look for, it would be so easy, said Hercule Poirot to himself. But one does not know what to look for. And so one looks in the wrong places or for the wrong things. He sighed vexedly. His eyes strayed from the jigsaw puzzle in front of him to the chair on the other side of the fireplace. There, not half an hour ago, Inspector Bland had sat consuming tea and crumpets (square crum-pets) and talking sadly. He had had to come to London on police business and that police business having been accom-plished, he had come to call upon M. Poirot. He had wondered, he explained, whether M. Poirot had any ideas. He had then proceeded to explain his own ideas. On every point he outlined, Poirot had agreed with him. Inspector Bland, so Poirot thought, had made a very fair and unprejudiced survey of the case.

It was now a month, nearly five weeks, since the occurrences at Nasse House. It had been five weeks of stagnation and of negation. Lady Stubbs' body had not been recovered. Lady Stubbs, if living, had not been traced. The odds, Inspector Bland pointed out, were strongly against her being alive. Poirot agreed with him.

'Of course,' said Bland, 'the body might not have been washed up. There's no telling with a body once it's in the water. It *may* show up yet, though it will be pretty unrecognizable when it does.'

'There is a third possibility,' Poirot pointed out.

Bland nodded.

'Yes,' he said, 'I've thought of that. I keep thinking of that, in fact. You mean the body's there—at Nasse, hidden somewhere where we've never thought of looking. It could be, you know. It just could be. With an old house, and with grounds like that, there are places you'd never think of—that you'd never know were there.'

He paused a moment, ruminated, and then said:

'There's a house I was in only the other day. They'd built an air-raid shelter, you know, in the war. A flimsy sort of more or less home-made job in the garden, by the wall of the house, and had made a way from it into the house—into the cellar. Well, the war ended, the shelters tumbled down, they heaped it up in irregular mounds and made a kind of rockery of it. Walking through that garden now, you'd never think that the place had once been an

air-raid shelter and that there was a chamber underneath. Looks as though it was always *meant* to be a rockery. And all the time, behind a wine bin in the cellar, there's a passage leading into it. That's what I mean. That kind of thing. Some sort of way into some kind of place that no outsider would know about. I don't suppose there's an actual Priest's Hole or anything of that kind?'

'Hardly—not at that period.'

'That's what Mr Weyman says—he says the house was built about 1790 or thereabouts. No reason for priests to hide themselves by that date. All the same, you know, there might be—somewhere, some alteration in the structure—something that one of the family might know about. What do you think, M. Poirot?'

'It is possible, yes,' said Poirot. '*Mais oui*, decidedly it is an idea. If one accepts the possibility, then the next thing is—who would know about it? Anyone staying in the house *might* know, I suppose?'

'Yes. Of course it would let out De Sousa.' The inspector looked dissatisfied. De Sousa was still his preferred suspect. 'As you say, anyone who lived in the house, such as a servant or one of the family, might know about it. Someone just staying in the house would be less likely. People who only came in from outside, like the Legges, less likely still.'

'The person who would certainly know about such a thing, and who could tell you if you asked her, would be Mrs Folliat,' said Poirot.

Mrs Folliat, he thought, knew all there was to know

about Nasse House. Mrs Folliat knew a great deal... Mrs Folliat had known straightaway that Hattie Stubbs was dead. Mrs Folliat knew, before Marlene and Hattie Stubbs died, that it was a very wicked world and that there were very wicked people in it. Mrs Folliat, thought Poirot vexedly, was the key to the whole business. But Mrs Folliat, he reflected, was a key that would not easily turn in the lock.

'I've interviewed the lady several times,' said the inspector. 'Very nice, very pleasant she's been about everything, and seems very distressed that she can't suggest anything helpful.'

Can't or won't? thought Poirot. Bland was perhaps thinking the same.

'There's a type of lady,' he said, 'that you can't force. You can't frighten them, or persuade them, or diddle them.'

No, Poirot thought, you couldn't force or persuade or diddle Mrs Folliat.

The inspector had finished his tea, and sighed and gone, and Poirot had got out his jigsaw puzzle to alleviate his mounting exasperation. For he was exasperated. Both exasperated and humiliated. Mrs Oliver had summoned him, Hercule Poirot, to elucidate a mystery. She had felt that there was something wrong, and there *had* been something wrong. And she had looked confidently to Hercule Poirot, first to prevent it—and he had not prevented it—and, secondly, to discover the killer, and he had *not* discovered the killer. He was in a fog, in the type of fog where there are from time to time baffling gleams of light. Every now and then, or so it seemed to him, he had had one of those glimpses. And each time he had failed to penetrate farther.

He had failed to assess the value of what he seemed, for one brief moment, to have seen.

Poirot got up, crossed to the other side of the hearth, rearranged the second square chair so that it was at a definite geometric angle, and sat down in it. He had passed from the jigsaw of painted wood and cardboard to the jigsaw of a murder problem. He took a notebook from his pocket and wrote in small neat characters:

'Etienne de Sousa, Amanda Brewis, Alec Legge, Sally Legge, Michael Weyman.'

It was physically impossible for Sir George or Jim Warburton to have killed Marlene Tucker. Since it was not physically impossible for Mrs Oliver to have done so, he added her name after a brief space. He also added the name of Mrs Masterton since he did not remember of his own knowledge having seen Mrs Masterton constantly on the lawn between four o'clock and quarter to five. He added the name of Henden, the butler; more, perhaps, because a sinister butler had figured in Mrs Oliver's Murder Hunt than because he had really any suspicions of the dark-haired artist with the gong stick. He also put down 'Boy in turtle shirt' with a query mark after it. Then he smiled, shook his head, took a pin from the lapel of his jacket, shut his eyes and stabbed with it. It was as good a way as any other, he thought.

He was justifiably annoyed when the pin proved to have transfixed the last entry.

'I am an imbecile,' said Hercule Poirot. 'What has a boy in a turtle shirt to do with this?'

But he also realized he must have had some reason for

including this enigmatic character in his list. He recalled again the day he had sat in the Folly, and the surprise on the boy's face at seeing him there. Not a very pleasant face, despite the youthful good looks. An arrogant ruthless face. The young man had come there for some purpose. He had come to meet someone, and it followed that that someone was a person whom he could not meet, or did not wish to meet, in the ordinary way. It was a meeting, in fact, to which attention must not be called. A guilty meeting. Something to do with the murder?

Poirot pursued his reflections. A boy who was staying at the Youth Hostel—that is to say, a boy who would be in that neighbourhood for two nights at most. Had he come there casually? One of the many young students visiting Britain? Or had he come there for a special purpose, to meet some special person? There could have been what seemed a casual encounter on the day of the fête—possibly there had been.

I know a good deal, said Hercule Poirot to himself. I have in my hands many, many pieces of this jigsaw. I have an idea of the *kind* of crime this was—but it must be that I am not looking at it the right way.

He turned a page of his notebook, and wrote:

Did Lady Stubbs ask Miss Brewis to take tea to Marlene?
If not, why does Miss Brewis say that she did?

He considered the point. Miss Brewis might quite easily herself have thought of taking cake and a fruit drink to the girl. But if so why did she not simply say so? Why lie about Lady Stubbs having asked her to do so? Could this be because Miss Brewis went to the boathouse *and found Marlene dead?* Unless Miss Brewis was herself guilty of the murder, that seemed very unlikely. She was not a nervous woman nor an imaginative one. If she had found the girl dead, she would surely at once have given the alarm?

He stared for some time at the two questions he had written. He could not help feeling that somewhere in those words there was some vital pointer to the truth that had escaped him. After four or five minutes of thought he wrote down something more.

Etienne de Sousa declares that he wrote to his cousin three weeks before his arrival at Nasse House. Is that statement true or false?

Poirot felt almost certain that it was false. He recalled the scene at the breakfast table. There seemed no earthly reason why Sir George or Lady Stubbs should pretend to a surprise and, in the latter's case, a dismay, which they did not feel. He could see no purpose to be accomplished by it. Granting, however, that Etienne de Sousa had lied, *why* did he lie? To give the impression that his visit had been announced and welcomed? It might be so, but it seemed a very doubtful reason. There was certainly no *evidence* that such a letter had ever been written or received. Was it an attempt on De Sousa's part to establish his *bona fides*—to make his visit appear natural and even expected? Certainly Sir George had received him amicably enough, although he did not know him.

Poirot paused, his thoughts coming to a stop. *Sir George did not know De Sousa. His wife, who did know him, had not seen him.* Was there perhaps something *there*? Could it be possible that the Etienne de Sousa who had arrived that day at the fête was not the real Etienne de Sousa? He went over the idea in his mind, but again he could see no point to it. What had De Sousa to gain by coming and representing himself as De Sousa if he was not De Sousa? In any case, De Sousa did not derive any benefit from Hattie's death. Hattie, as the police had ascertained, had no money of her own except that which was allowed her by her husband.

Poirot tried to remember exactly what she had said to him that morning. 'He is a bad man. He does wicked things.' And, according to Bland, she had said to her husband: 'He kills people.'

There was something rather significant about that, now that one came to examine all the facts. *He kills people.*

On the day Etienne de Sousa had come to Nasse House one person certainly had been killed, possibly two people. Mrs Folliat had said that one should pay no attention to these melodramatic remarks of Hattie's. She had said so very insistently. Mrs Folliat...

Hercule Poirot frowned, then brought his hand down with a bang on the arm of his chair.

'Always, always—I return to Mrs Folliat. She is the key to the whole business. If I knew what she knows... I can no longer sit in an armchair and just think. No, I must take a train and go again to Devon and visit Mrs Folliat.'

II

Hercule Poirot paused for a moment outside the big wrought-iron gates of Nasse House. He looked ahead of him along the curving drive. It was no longer summer. Golden-brown leaves fluttered gently down from the trees. Near at hand the grassy banks were coloured with small mauve cyclamen. Poirot sighed. The beauty of Nasse House appealed to him in spite of himself. He was not a great admirer of nature in the wild, he liked things trim and neat, yet he could not but appreciate the soft wild beauty of massed shrubs and trees.

At his left was the small white porticoed lodge. It was a fine afternoon. Probably Mrs Folliat would not be at home. She would be out somewhere with her gardening basket or else visiting some friends in the neighbourhood. She had many friends. This was her home, and had been her home for many long years. What was it the old man on the quay had said? 'There'll always be Folliats at Nasse House.'

Poirot rapped gently upon the door of the Lodge. After a few moments' delay he heard footsteps inside. They sounded to his ear slow and almost hesitant. Then the door was opened and Mrs Folliat stood framed in the doorway. He was startled to see how old and frail she looked. She stared at him incredulously for a moment or two, then she said:

'M. Poirot? You!'

He thought for a moment that he had seen fear leap into her eyes, but perhaps that was sheer imagination on his part. He said politely:

'May I come in, Madame?'

'But of course.'

She had recovered all her poise now, beckoned him in with a gesture and led the way into her small sitting-room. There were some delicate Chelsea figures on the mantelpiece, a couple of chairs covered in exquisite petit point, and a Derby tea service stood on the small table. Mrs Folliat said:

'I will fetch another cup.'

Poirot raised a faintly protesting hand, but she pushed the protest aside.

'Of course you must have some tea.'

She went out of the room. He looked round him once more. A piece of needlework, a petit point chair seat, lay on a table with a needle sticking in it. Against the wall was a bookcase with books. There was a little cluster of miniatures on the wall and a faded photograph in a silver frame of a man in uniform with a stiff moustache and a weak chin.

Mrs Folliat came back into the room with a cup and saucer in her hand.

Poirot said, 'Your husband, Madame?'

'Yes.'

Noticing that Poirot's eyes swept along the top of the bookcase as though in search of further photographs, she said brusquely:

'I'm not fond of photographs. They make one live in the past too much. One must learn to forget. One must cut away the dead wood.'

Poirot remembered how the first time he had seen Mrs Folliat she had been clipping with secateurs at a shrub on the bank. She had said then, he remembered, something about dead wood. He looked at her thoughtfully, appraising her character. An enigmatical woman, he thought, and a woman who, in spite of the gentleness and fragility of her appearance, had a side to her that could be ruthless. A woman who could cut away dead wood not only from plants but from her own life...

She sat down and poured out a cup of tea, asking: 'Milk? Sugar?'

'Three lumps if you will be so good, Madame?'

She handed him his cup and said conversationally:

'I was surprised to see you. Somehow I did not imagine you would be passing through this part of the world again.'

'I am not exactly passing through,' said Poirot.

'No?' She queried him with slightly uplifted eyebrows.

'My visit to this part of the world is intentional.'

She still looked at him in inquiry.

'I came here partly to see you, Madame.'

'Really?'

'First of all—there has been no news of the young Lady Stubbs?'

Mrs Folliat shook her head.

'There was a body washed up the other day in Cornwall,' she said. 'George went there to see if he could identify it. But it was not her.' She added: 'I am very sorry for George. The strain has been very great.'

'Does he still believe that his wife may be alive?'

Slowly Mrs Folliat shook her head.

'I think,' she said, 'that he has given up hope. After all, if

Hattie were alive, she couldn't possibly conceal herself successfully with the whole of the Press and the police looking for her. Even if something like loss of memory had happened to her—well, surely the police would have found her by now?'

'It would seem so, yes,' said Poirot. 'Do the police still search?'

'I suppose so. I do not really know.'

'But Sir George has given up hope.'

'He does not say so,' said Mrs Folliat. 'Of course I have not seen him lately. He has been mostly in London.'

'And the murdered girl? There have been no developments there?'

'Not that I know of.' She added. 'It seems a senseless crime—absolutely pointless. Poor child—'

'It still upsets you, I see, to think of her, Madame.'

Mrs Folliat did not reply for a moment or two. Then she said:

'I think when one is old, the death of anyone who is young upsets one out of due proportion. We old folks expect to die, but that child had her life before her.'

'It might not have been a very interesting life.'

'Not from our point of view, perhaps, but it might have been interesting to her.'

'And although, as you say, we old folk must expect to die,' said Poirot, 'we do not really want to. At least *I* do not want to. I find life very interesting still.'

'I don't think that I do.'

She spoke more to herself than him, her shoulders drooped still more.

'I am very tired, M. Poirot. I shall be not only ready, but thankful, when my time comes.'

He shot a quick glance at her. He wondered, as he had wondered before, whether it was a sick woman who sat talking to him, a woman who had perhaps the knowledge or even the certainty of approaching death. He could not otherwise account for the intense weariness and lassitude of her manner. That lassitude, he felt, was not really characteristic of the woman. Amy Folliat, he felt, was a woman of character, energy and determination. She had lived through many troubles, loss of her home, loss of wealth, the deaths of her sons. All these, he felt, she had survived. She had cut away the 'dead wood,' as she herself had expressed it. But there was something now in her life that she could not cut away, that no one could cut away for her. If it was not physical illness he did not see what it could be. She gave a sudden little smile as though she were reading his thoughts.

'Really, you know, I have not very much to live for, M. Poirot,' she said. 'I have many friends but no near relations, no family.'

'You have your home,' said Poirot on an impulse.

'You mean Nasse? Yes—'

'It is *your* home, isn't it, although technically it is the property of Sir George Stubbs? Now Sir George Stubbs has gone to London you rule in his stead.'

Again he saw the sharp look of fear in her eyes. When she spoke her voice held an icy edge to it.

'I don't quite know what you mean, M. Poirot. I am grateful to Sir George for renting me this lodge, but I *do* rent it. I pay him a yearly sum for it with the right to walk in the grounds.'

Poirot spread out his hands.

'I apologize, Madame. I did not mean to offend you.'

'No doubt I misunderstood you,' said Mrs Folliat coldly.

'It is a beautiful place,' said Poirot. 'A beautiful house, beautiful grounds. It has about it a great peace, great serenity.'

'Yes.' Her face lightened. 'We have always felt that. I felt it as a child when I first came here.'

'But is there the same peace and serenity *now*, Madame?'

'Why not?'

'Murder unavenged,' said Poirot. 'The spilling of innocent blood. Until that shadow lifts, there will not be peace.' He added, 'I think you know that, Madame, as well as I do.'

Mrs Folliat did not answer. She neither moved nor spoke. She sat quite still and Poirot had no idea what she was thinking. He leaned forward a little and spoke again.

'Madame, you know a good deal—perhaps everything— about this murder. You know who killed that girl, you know *why*. You know who killed Hattie Stubbs, you know, perhaps, where her body lies now.'

Mrs Folliat spoke then. Her voice was loud, almost harsh.

'I know nothing,' she said. '*Nothing*.'

'Perhaps I have used the wrong word. You do not know, but I think you *guess*, Madame. I'm quite sure that you guess.'

'Now you are being—excuse me—absurd!'

'It is not absurd—it is something quite different—it is *dangerous*.'

'Dangerous? To whom?'

'To you, Madame. So long as you keep your knowledge to yourself you are in danger. I know murderers better than you do, Madame.'

'I have told you already, I have no knowledge.'

'Suspicions, then—'

'I have no suspicions.'

'That, excuse me, is not true, Madame.'

'To speak out of mere suspicion would be wrong—indeed, wicked.'

Poirot leaned forward. 'As wicked as what was done here just over a month ago?'

She shrank back into her chair, huddled into herself. She half whispered:

'Don't talk to me of it.' And then added, with a long shuddering sigh, 'Anyway, it's over now. Done—finished with.'

'How can you tell that, Madame? I tell you of my own knowledge that it is *never* finished with a murderer.'

She shook her head.

'No. No, it's the end. And, anyway, there is nothing *I* can do. Nothing.'

He got up and stood looking down at her. She said almost fretfully:

'Why, even the police have given up.'

Poirot shook his head.

'Oh, no, Madame, you are wrong there. The police do not give up. And I,' he added, 'do not give up either. Remember that, Madame, I, Hercule Poirot, do not give up.'

It was a very typical exit line.

CHAPTER 17

After leaving Nasse, Poirot went to the village where, by inquiry, he found the cottage occupied by the Tuckers. His knock at the door went unanswered for some moments as it was drowned by the high-pitched tone of Mrs Tucker's voice from inside.

'—And what be yu thinking of, Jim Tucker, bringing them boots of yours on to my nice linoleum? If I've tell ee once I've tell ee a thousand times. Been polishing it all the morning, I have, and now look at it.'

A faint rumbling denoted Mr Tucker's reaction to these remarks. It was on the whole a placatory rumble.

'Yu've no cause to go forgetting. 'Tis all this eagerness to get the sports news on the wireless. Why, 'twouldn't have took ee tu minutes to be off with them boots. And yu, Gary, do ee mind what yu'm doing with that lollipop. Sticky fingers I will not have on my best silver teapot. Marilyn, that be someone at the door, that be. Du ee go and see who 'tis.'

The door was opened gingerly and a child of about eleven or twelve years old peered out suspiciously at Poirot. One cheek was bulged with a sweet. She was a fat child with small blue eyes and a rather piggy kind of prettiness.

''Tis a gentleman, Mum,' she shouted.

Mrs Tucker, wisps of hair hanging over her somewhat hot face, came to the door.

'What is it?' she demanded sharply. 'We don't need...' She paused, a faint look of recognition came across her face. 'Why let me see, now, didn't I see you with the police that day?'

'Alas, Madame, that I have brought back painful memories,' said Poirot, stepping firmly inside the door.

Mrs Tucker cast a swift agonized glance at his feet, but Poirot's pointed patent-leather shoes had only trodden the high road. No mud was being deposited on Mrs Tucker's brightly polished linoleum.

'Come in, won't you, sir,' she said, backing before him, and throwing open the door of a room on her right hand.

Poirot was ushered into a devastatingly neat little parlour. It smelt of furniture polish and Brasso and contained a large Jacobean suite, a round table, two potted geraniums, an elaborate brass fender, and a large variety of china ornaments.

'Sit down, sir, do. I can't remember the name. Indeed, I don't think as I ever heard it.'

'My name is Hercule Poirot,' said Poirot rapidly. 'I found myself once more in this part of the world and I called here to offer you my condolences and to ask you if there

202

had been any developments. I trust the murderer of your daughter has been discovered.'

'Not sight or sound of him,' said Mrs Tucker, speaking with some bitterness. 'And 'tis a downright wicked shame if you ask me. 'Tis my opinion the police don't disturb themselves when it's only the likes of us. What's the police anyway? If they'm all like Bob Hoskins I wonder the whole country isn't a mass of crime. All that Bob Hoskins does is spend his time looking into parked cars on the Common.'

At this point, Mr Tucker, his boots removed, appeared through the doorway, walking on his stockinged feet. He was a large, red-faced man with a pacific expression.

'Police be all right,' he said in a husky voice. 'Got their troubles like anyone else. These here maniacs ar'n't so easy to find. Look the same as you or me, if you take my meaning,' he added, speaking directly to Poirot.

The little girl who had opened the door to Poirot appeared behind her father, and a boy of about eight poked his head round her shoulder. They all stared at Poirot with intense interest.

'This is your younger daughter, I suppose,' said Poirot.

'That's Marilyn, that is,' said Mrs Tucker. 'And that's Gary. Come and say how do you do, Gary, and mind your manners.'

Gary backed away.

'Shy-like, he is,' said his mother.

'Very civil of you, I'm sure, sir,' said Mr Tucker, 'to come and ask about Marlene. Ah, that was a terrible business, to be sure.'

'I have just called upon Mrs Folliat,' said M. Poirot. 'She, too, seems to feel this very deeply.'

'She's been poorly-like ever since,' said Mrs Tucker. 'She's an old lady an't was a shock to her, happening as it did at her own place.'

Poirot noted once more everybody's unconscious assumption that Nasse House still belonged to Mrs Folliat.

'Makes her feel responsible-like in a way,' said Mr Tucker, 'not that 'twere anything to do with her.'

'Who was it that actually suggested that Marlene should play the victim?' asked Poirot.

'The lady from London that writes the books,' said Mrs Tucker promptly.

Poirot said mildly:

'But she was a stranger down here. She did not even know Marlene.'

''Twas Mrs Masterton what rounded the girls up,' said Mrs Tucker, 'and I suppose 'twas Mrs Masterton said Marlene was to do it. And Marlene, I must say, was pleased enough at the idea.'

Once again, Poirot felt, he came up against a blank wall. But he knew now what Mrs Oliver had felt when she first sent for him. Someone had been working in the dark, someone who had pushed forward their own desires through other recognized personalities. Mrs Oliver, Mrs Masterton. Those were the figureheads. He said:

'I have been wondering, Mrs Tucker, whether Marlene was already acquainted with this—er—homicidal maniac.'

'She wouldn't know nobody like that,' said Mrs Tucker virtuously.

'Ah,' said Poirot, 'but as your husband has just observed, these maniacs are very difficult to spot. They look the same as—er—you and me. Someone may have spoken to Marlene at the fête, or even before it. Made friends with her in a perfectly harmless manner. Given her presents, perhaps.'

'Oh, no, sir, nothing of that kind. Marlene wouldn't take presents from a stranger. I brought her up better than that.'

'But she might see no harm in it,' said Poirot, persisting. 'Supposing it had been some nice lady who had offered her things.'

'Someone, you mean, like young Mrs Legge down at the Mill Cottage.'

'Yes,' said Poirot. 'Someone like that.'

'Give Marlene a lipstick once, she did,' said Mrs Tucker. 'Ever so mad, I was. I won't have you putting that muck on your face, Marlene, I said. Think what your father would say. Well, she says, perky as may be, 'tis the lady down at Lawder's Cottage as give it me. Said as how it would suit me, she did. Well, I said, don't you listen to what no London ladies say. 'Tis all very well for *them*, painting their faces and blacking their eyelashes and everything else. But you're a decent girl, I said, and you wash your face with soap and water until you're a good deal older than what you are now.'

'But she did not agree with you, I expect,' said Poirot, smiling.

'When I say a thing I mean it,' said Mrs Tucker.

The fat Marilyn suddenly gave an amused giggle. Poirot shot her a keen glance.

'Did Mrs Legge give Marlene anything else?' he asked.

'Believe she gave her a scarf or summat—one she hadn't no more use for. A showy sort of thing, but not much quality. I know quality when I see it,' said Mrs Tucker, nodding her head. 'Used to work at Nasse House as a girl, I did. Proper stuff the ladies wore in those days. No gaudy colours and all this nylon and rayon; real good silk. Why, some of their taffeta dresses would have stood up by themselves.'

'Girls like a bit of finery,' said Mr Tucker indulgently. 'I don't mind a few bright colours myself, but I won't have this 'ere mucky lipstick.'

'A bit sharp I was with her,' said Mrs Tucker, her eyes suddenly misty, 'and her gorn in that terrible way. Wished afterwards I hadn't spoken so sharp. Ah, nought but trouble and funerals lately, it seems. Troubles never come singly, so they say, and 'tis true enough.'

'You have had other losses?' inquired Poirot politely.

'The wife's father,' explained Mr Tucker. 'Come across the ferry in his boat from the Three Dogs late at night, and must have missed his footing getting on to the quay and fallen in the river. Of course he ought to have stayed quiet at home at his age. But there, yu can't do anything with the old 'uns. Always pottering about on the quay, he was.'

'Father was a great one for the boats always,' said Mrs Tucker. 'Used to look after them in the old days for Mr Folliat, years and years ago that was. Not,' she added brightly, 'as Father's much loss, as you might say. Well over ninety, he was, and trying in many of his ways. Always babbling some nonsense or other. 'Twas time he went. But, of course, us had to bury him nice—and two funerals running costs a lot of money.'

These economic reflections passed Poirot by—a faint remembrance was stirring.

'An old man—on the quay? I remember talking to him. Was his name—?'

'Merdell, sir. That was my name before I married.'

'Your father, if I remember rightly, was head gardener at Nasse?'

'No, that was my eldest brother. I was the youngest of the family—eleven of us, there were.' She added with some pride, 'There's been Merdells at Nasse for years, but they're all scattered now. Father was the last of us.'

Poirot said softly:

'There'll always be Folliats at Nasse House.'

'I beg your pardon, sir?'

'I am repeating what your old father said to me on the quay.'

'Ah, talked a lot of nonsense, Father did. I had to shut him up pretty sharp now and then.'

'So Marlene was Merdell's granddaughter,' said Poirot. 'Yes, I begin to see.' He was silent for a moment, an immense excitement was surging within him. 'Your father was drowned, you say, in the river?'

'Yes, sir. Took a drop too much, he did. And where he got the money from, I don't know. Of course he used to get tips now and again on the quay helping people with boats or with parking their cars. Very cunning he was at hiding his money from me. Yes, I'm afraid as he'd had a drop too much. Missed his footing, I'd say, getting off his boat on to the quay. So he fell in and was drowned. His body was washed up down at Helmmouth the next day. 'Tis a wonder, as you might say, that it never happened before, him being ninety-two and half blinded anyway.'

'The fact remains that it did *not* happen before—'

'Ah, well, accidents happen, sooner or later—'

'Accident,' mused Poirot. 'I wonder.'

He got up. He murmured:

'I should have guessed. Guessed long ago. The child practically told me—'

'I beg your pardon, sir?'

'It is nothing,' said Poirot. 'Once more I tender you my condolences both on the death of your daughter and on that of your father.'

He shook hands with them both and left the cottage. He said to himself:

'I have been foolish—very foolish. I have looked at everything the wrong way round.'

'Hi—mister.'

It was a cautious whisper. Poirot looked round. The fat child Marilyn was standing in the shadow of the cottage wall. She beckoned him to her and spoke in a whisper.

'Mum don't know everything,' she said. 'Marlene didn't get that scarf off of the lady down at the cottage.'

'Where did she get it?'

208

'Bought it in Torquay. Bought some lipstick, too, and some scent—Newt in Paris—funny name. And a jar of foundation cream, what she'd read about in an advertisement.' Marilyn giggled. 'Mum doesn't know. Hid it at the back of her drawer, Marlene did, under her winter vests. Used to go into the convenience at the bus stop and do herself up, when she went to the pictures.'

Marilyn giggled again.

'Mum never knew.'

'Didn't your mother find these things after your sister died?'

Marilyn shook her fair fluffy head.

'No,' she said. 'I got 'em now—in my drawer. Mum doesn't know.'

Poirot eyed her consideringly, and said:

'You seem a very clever girl, Marilyn.'

Marilyn grinned rather sheepishly.

'Miss Bird says it's no good my trying for the grammar school.'

'Grammar school is not everything,' said Poirot. 'Tell me, how did Marlene get the money to buy these things?'

Marilyn looked with close attention at a drain-pipe.

'Dunno,' she muttered.

'I think you do know,' said Poirot.

Shamelessly he drew out a half-crown from his pocket and added another half-crown to it.

'I believe,' he said, 'there is a new, very attractive shade of lipstick called "Carmine Kiss."'

'Sounds smashing,' said Marilyn, her hand advanced

209

towards the five shillings. She spoke in a rapid whisper. 'She used to snoop about a bit, Marlene did. Used to see goings-on—you know what. Marlene would promise not to tell and then they'd give her a present, see?'

Poirot relinquished the five shillings.

'I see,' he said.

He nodded to Marilyn and walked away. He murmured again under his breath, but this time with intensified meaning:

'I see.'

So many things now fell into place. Not all of it. Not clear yet by any means—but he was on the right track. A perfectly clear trail all the way if only he had had the wit to see it. That first conversation with Mrs Oliver, some casual words of Michael Weyman's, the significant conversation with old Merdell on the quay, an illuminating phrase spoken by Miss Brewis—the arrival of Etienne de Sousa.

A public telephone box stood adjacent to the village post office. He entered it and rang up a number. A few minutes later he was speaking to Inspector Bland.

'Well, M. Poirot, where are you?'

'I am here, in Nassecombe.'

'But you were in London yesterday afternoon?'

'It only takes three and a half hours to come here by a good train,' Poirot pointed out. 'I have a question for you.'

'Yes?'

'What kind of a yacht did Etienne de Sousa have?'

'Maybe I can guess what you're thinking, M. Poirot, but I assure you there was nothing of that kind. It wasn't fitted

210

up for smuggling if that's what you mean. There were no fancy hidden partitions or secret cubby-holes. We'd have found them if there had been. There was nowhere on it you could have stowed away a body.'

'You are wrong, *mon cher*, that is not what I mean. I only asked what kind of yacht, big or small?'

'Oh, it was very fancy. Must have cost the earth. All very smart, newly painted, luxury fittings.'

'Exactly,' said Poirot. He sounded so pleased that Inspector Bland felt quite surprised.

'What are you getting at, M. Poirot?' he asked.

'Etienne de Sousa,' said Poirot, 'is a rich man. That, my friend, is very significant.'

'Why?' demanded Inspector Bland.

'It fits in with my latest idea,' said Poirot.

'You've got an idea, then?'

'Yes. At last I have an idea. Up to now I have been very stupid.'

'You mean we've all been very stupid.'

'No,' said Poirot, 'I mean specially myself. I had the good fortune to have a perfectly clear trail presented to me, and I did not see it.'

'But now you're definitely on to something?'

'I think so, yes.'

'Look here, M. Poirot—'

But Poirot had rung off. After searching his pockets for available change, he put through a personal call to Mrs Oliver at her London number.

'But do not,' he hastened to add, when he made his

demand, 'disturb the lady to answer the telephone if she is at work.'

He remembered how bitterly Mrs Oliver had once reproached him for interrupting a train of creative thought and how the world in consequence had been deprived of an intriguing mystery centring round an old-fashioned long-sleeved woollen vest. The exchange, however, was unable to appreciate his scruples.

'Well,' it demanded, 'do you want a personal call or don't you?'

'I do,' said Poirot, sacrificing Mrs Oliver's creative genius upon the altar of his own impatience. He was relieved when Mrs Oliver spoke. She interrupted his apologies.

'It's splendid that you've rung me up,' she said. 'I was just going out to give a talk on *How I Write My Books*. Now I can get my secretary to ring up and say I am un-avoidably detained.'

'But, Madame, you must not let me prevent—'

'It's not a case of preventing,' said Mrs Oliver joyfully. 'I'd have made the most awful fool of myself. I mean, what *can* you say about how you write books? What I mean is, first you've got to think of something, and when you've thought of it you've got to force yourself to sit down and write it. That's all. It would have taken me just three minutes to explain that, and then the Talk would have been ended and everyone would have been very fed up. I can't imagine why everybody is always so keen for authors to *talk* about writing. I should have thought it was an author's business to *write*, not *talk*.'

'And yet it is about how you write that I want to ask you.'

'You can ask,' said Mrs Oliver; 'but I probably shan't know the answer. I mean one just sits down and writes. Half a minute, I've got a frightfully silly hat on for the Talk—and I *must* take it off. It scratches my forehead.' There was a momentary pause and then the voice of Mrs Oliver resumed in a relieved voice, 'Hats are really only a symbol, nowadays, aren't they? I mean, one doesn't wear them for sensible reasons any more; to keep one's head warm, or shield one from the sun, or hide one's face from people one doesn't want to meet. I beg your pardon, M. Poirot, did you say something?'

'It was an ejaculation only. It is extraordinary,' said Poirot, and his voice was awed. 'Always you give me ideas. So also did my friend Hastings whom I have not seen for many, many years. You have given me now the clue to yet another piece of my problem. But no more of all that. Let me ask you instead my question. Do you know an atom scientist, Madame?'

'Do I know an atom scientist?' said Mrs Oliver in a surprised voice. 'I don't know. I suppose I *may*. I mean, I know some professors and things. I'm never quite sure what they actually *do*.'

'Yet you made an atom scientist one of the suspects in your Murder Hunt?'

'Oh, *that*! That was just to be up to date. I mean, when I went to buy presents for my nephews last Christmas, there was nothing but science fiction and the stratosphere and supersonic toys, and so I thought when I started on the Murder Hunt, "Better have an atom scientist as the chief suspect and be modern." After all, if I'd needed a little technical jargon for it I could always have got it from Alec Legge.'

'Alec Legge—the husband of Sally Legge? Is he an atom scientist?'

'Yes, he is. Not Harwell. Wales somewhere. Cardiff. Or Bristol, is it? It's just a holiday cottage they have on the Helm. Yes, so, of course, I *do* know an atom scientist after all.'

'And it was meeting him at Nasse House that probably put the idea of an atom scientist into your head? But his wife is not Yugoslavian.'

'Oh, *no*,' said Mrs Oliver, 'Sally is English as English. Surely you realize *that*?'

'Then what put the idea of the Yugoslavian wife into your head?'

'I really don't know... Refugees perhaps? Students? All those foreign girls at the hostel trespassing through the woods and speaking broken English.'

'I see... Yes, I see now a lot of things.'

'It's about time,' said Mrs Oliver.

'*Pardon?*'

'I said it was about time,' said Mrs Oliver. 'That you did see things, I mean. Up to now you don't seem to have done *anything*.' Her voice held reproach.

'One cannot arrive at things all in a moment,' said Poirot, defending himself. 'The police,' he added, 'have been completely baffled.'

'Oh, the police,' said Mrs Oliver. 'Now if a woman were the head of Scotland Yard...'

Recognizing this well-known phrase, Poirot hastened to interrupt.

'The matter has been complex,' he said. 'Extremely complex. But now—I tell you this in confidence—but now I arrive!'

Mrs Oliver remained unimpressed.

'I dare say,' she said; 'but in the meantime there have been two murders.'

'Three,' Poirot corrected her.

'Three murders? Who's the third?'

'An old man called Merdell,' said Hercule Poirot.

'I haven't heard of that one,' said Mrs Oliver. 'Will it be in the paper?'

'No,' said Poirot, 'up to now no one has suspected that it was anything but an accident.'

'And it wasn't an accident?'

'No,' said Poirot, 'it was not an accident.'

'Well, tell me who did it—did them, I mean—or can't you over the telephone?'

'One does not say these things over the telephone,' said Poirot.

'Then I shall ring off,' said Mrs Oliver. 'I can't bear it.'

'Wait a moment,' said Poirot, 'there is something else I wanted to ask you. Now, what was it?'

'That's a sign of age,' said Mrs Oliver. 'I do that, too. Forget things—'

'There was something, some little point—it worried me. I was in the boathouse...'

He cast his mind back. That pile of comics. Marlene's phrases scrawled on the margin. 'Albert goes with Doreen.' He had had a feeling that there was something lacking—that there was something he must ask Mrs Oliver.

'Are you still there, M. Poirot?' demanded Mrs Oliver. At the same time the operator requested more money.

These formalities completed, Poirot spoke once more.

'Are you still there, Madame?'

'*I'm* still here,' said Mrs Oliver. 'Don't let's waste any more money asking each other if we're there. What is it?'

'It is something very important. You remember your Murder Hunt?'

'Well, of course I remember it. It's practically what we've just been talking about, isn't it?'

'I made one grave mistake,' said Poirot. 'I never read your synopsis for competitors. In the gravity of discovering a murder it did not seem to matter. I was wrong. It did matter. You are a sensitive person, Madame. You are affected by your atmosphere, by the personalities of the people you meet. And these are translated into your work. Not recognizably so, but they are the inspiration from which your fertile brain draws its creations.'

'That's very nice flowery language,' said Mrs Oliver. 'But what exactly do you mean?'

'That you have always known more about this crime than you have realized yourself. Now for the question I want to ask you—two questions actually; but the first is very important. Did you, when you first began to plan your Murder Hunt, mean the body to be discovered in the boathouse?'

'No, I didn't.'

'Where did you intend it to be?'

'In that funny little summer-house tucked away in the rhododendrons near the house. I thought it was just the place. But then someone, I can't remember who exactly, began insisting that it should be found in the Folly. Well, that, of course, was an *absurd* idea! I mean, anyone could have strolled in there quite casually and come across it without having followed a single clue. People are so stupid. Of course I couldn't agree to *that*.'

'So, instead, you accepted the boathouse?'

'Yes, that's just how it happened. There was really nothing against the boathouse though I still thought the little summer-house would have been better.'

'Yes, that is the technique you outlined to me that first day. There is one thing more. Do you remember telling me that there was a final clue written on one of the "comics" that Marlene was given to amuse her?'

'Yes, of course.'

'Tell me, was it something like' (he forced his memory back to a moment when he had stood reading various scrawled phrases): 'Albert goes with Doreen; Georgie Porgie kisses hikers in the wood; Peter pinches girls in the Cinema?'

'Good gracious me, no,' said Mrs Oliver in a slightly shocked voice. 'It wasn't anything silly like that. No, mine was a perfectly straightforward clue.' She lowered her voice and spoke in mysterious tones. '*Look in the hiker's rucksack*.'

'*Epatant!*' cried Poirot. '*Epatant!* Of course, the "comic"

217

with that on it would *have* to be taken away. It might have given someone ideas!'

'The rucksack, of course, was on the floor by the body and—'

'Ah, but it is another rucksack of which I am thinking.'

'You're confusing me with all these rucksacks,' Mrs Oliver complained. 'There was only one in my murder story. Don't you want to know what was in it?'

'Not in the least,' said Poirot. 'That is to say,' he added politely, 'I should be enchanted to hear, of course, but—'

Mrs Oliver swept over the 'but.'

'Very ingenious, *I* think,' she said, the pride of authorship in her voice. 'You see, in Marlene's haversack, which was supposed to be the Yugoslavian wife's haversack, if you understand what I mean—'

'Yes, yes,' said Poirot, preparing himself to be lost in fog once more.

'Well, in it was the bottle of medicine containing poison with which the country squire poisoned his wife. You see, the Yugoslavian girl had been over here training as a nurse and she'd been in the house when Colonel Blunt poisoned his first wife for her money. And she, the nurse, had got hold of the bottle and taken it away, and then come back to blackmail him. That, of course, is why he killed her. Does that fit in, M. Poirot?'

'Fit in with what?'

'With your ideas,' said Mrs Oliver.

'Not at all,' said Poirot, but added hastily, 'All the same,

218

my felicitations, Madame. I am sure your Murder Hunt was so ingenious that nobody won the prize.'

'But they did,' said Mrs Oliver. 'Quite late, about seven o'clock. A very dogged old lady supposed to be quite gaga. She got through all the clues and arrived at the boathouse triumphantly, but of course the police were there. So then she heard about the murder, and she was the last person at the whole fête to hear about it, I should imagine. Anyway, they gave her the prize.' She added with satisfaction, 'That horrid young man with the freckles who said I drank like a fish never got farther than the camellia garden.'

'Some day, Madame,' said Poirot, 'you shall tell me this story of yours.'

'Actually,' said Mrs Oliver, 'I'm thinking of turning it into a book. It would be a pity to waste it.'

And it may here be mentioned that some three years later Hercule Poirot read *The Woman in the Wood*, by Ariadne Oliver, and wondered whilst he read it why some of the persons and incidents seemed to him vaguely familiar.

CHAPTER 18

The sun was setting when Poirot came to what was called officially Mill Cottage, and known locally as the Pink Cottage down by Lawder's Creek. He knocked on the door and it was flung open with such suddenness that he started back. The angry-looking young man in the doorway stared at him for a moment without recognizing him. Then he gave a short laugh.

'Hallo,' he said, 'it's the sleuth. Come in, M. Poirot. I'm packing up.'

Poirot accepted the invitation and stepped into the cottage. It was plainly, rather badly furnished. And Alec Legge's personal possessions were at the moment taking up a disproportionate amount of room. Books, papers and articles of stray clothing were strewn all around, an open suitcase stood on the floor.

'The final break-up of the *ménage*,' said Alec Legge. 'Sally has cleared out. I expect you know that.'

'I did not know it, no.'

Alec Legge gave a short laugh.

'I'm glad there's something you don't know. Yes, she's had enough of married life. Going to link up her life with that tame architect.'

'I am sorry to hear it,' said Poirot.

'I don't see why you should be sorry.'

'I am sorry,' said Poirot, clearing off two books and a shirt and sitting down on the corner of the sofa, 'because I do not think she will be as happy with him as she would be with you.'

'She hasn't been particularly happy with me this last six months.'

'Six months is not a lifetime,' said Poirot, 'it is a very short space out of what might be a long happy married life.'

'Talking rather like a parson, aren't you?'

'Possibly. May I say, Mr Legge, that if your wife has not been happy with you it is probably more your fault than hers.'

'She certainly thinks so. Everything's my fault, I suppose.'

'Not everything, but some things.'

'Oh, blame everything on me. I might as well drown myself in the damn' river and have done with it.'

Poirot looked at him thoughtfully.

'I am glad to observe,' he remarked, 'that you are now more perturbed with your own troubles than with those of the world.'

'The world can go hang,' said Mr Legge. He added bitterly, 'I seem to have made the most complete fool of myself all along the line.'

'Yes,' said Poirot, 'I would say that you have been more unfortunate than reprehensible in your conduct.'

Alec Legge stared at him.

'Who hired you to sleuth me?' he demanded. 'Was it Sally?'

'Why should you think that?'

'Well, nothing's happened officially. So I concluded that you must have come down after me on a private job.'

'You are in error,' replied Poirot. 'I have not at any time been sleuthing you. When I came down here I had no idea that you existed.'

'Then how do you know whether I've been unfortunate or made a fool of myself or what?'

'From the result of observation and reflection,' said Poirot. 'Shall I make a little guess and will you tell me if I am right?'

'You can make as many little guesses as you like,' said Alec Legge. 'But don't expect me to play.'

'I think,' said Poirot, 'that some years ago you had an interest and sympathy for a certain political party. Like many other young men of a scientific bent. In your profession such sympathies and tendencies are naturally regarded with suspicion. I do not think you were ever seriously compromised, but I *do* think that pressure was brought upon you to consolidate your position in a way you did not want to consolidate it. You tried to withdraw and you were faced with a threat. You were given a rendezvous with someone. I doubt if I shall ever know that young man's name. He will be for me always *the young man in a turtle shirt*.'

222

Alec Legge gave a sudden explosion of laughter.

'I suppose that shirt was a bit of a joke. I wasn't seeing things very funny at the time.'

Hercule Poirot continued.

'What with worry over the fate of the world, and the worry over your own predicament, you became, if I may say so, a man almost impossible for any woman to live with happily. You did not confide in your wife. That was unfortunate for you, as I should say that your wife was a woman of loyalty, and that if she had realized how unhappy and desperate you were, she would have been whole-heartedly on your side. Instead of that she merely began to compare you, unfavourably, with a former friend of hers, Michael Weyman.'

He rose.

'I should advise you, Mr Legge, to complete your packing as soon as possible, to follow your wife to London, to ask her to forgive you and to tell her all that you have been through.'

'So that's what you advise,' said Alec Legge. 'And what the hell business is it of yours?'

'None,' said Hercule Poirot. He withdrew towards the door. 'But I am always right.'

There was a moment's silence. Then Alec Legge burst into a wild peal of laughter.

'Do you know,' he said, 'I think I'll take your advice. Divorce is damned expensive. Anyway, if you've got hold of the woman you want, and are then not able to keep her, it's a bit humiliating, don't you think? I shall go up to her flat in Chelsea, and if I find Michael there I shall take hold of him by that hand-knitted pansy tie he wears and throttle the life out of him. I'd enjoy that. Yes, I'd enjoy it a good deal.'

His face suddenly lit up with a most attractive smile.

'Sorry for my filthy temper,' he said, 'and thanks a lot.'

He clapped Poirot on the shoulder. With the force of the blow Poirot staggered and all but fell.

Mr Legge's friendship was certainly more painful than his animosity.

'And now,' said Poirot, leaving Mill Cottage on painful feet and looking up at the darkening sky, 'where do I go?'

CHAPTER 19

The chief constable and Inspector Bland looked up with keen curiosity as Hercule Poirot was ushered in. The chief constable was not in the best of tempers. Only Bland's quiet persistence had caused him to cancel his dinner appointment for that evening.

'I know, Bland, I know,' he said fretfully. 'Maybe he was a little Belgian wizard in his day—but surely, man, his day's over. He's what age?'

Bland slid tactfully over the answer to this question which, in any case, he did not know. Poirot himself was always reticent on the subject of his age.

'The point is, sir, he was *there*—on the spot. And we're not getting anywhere any other way. Up against a blank wall, that's where we are.'

The chief constable blew his nose irritably.

'I know. I know. Makes me begin to believe in Mrs Masterton's homicidal pervert. I'd even use bloodhounds, if there were anywhere to use them.'

'Bloodhounds can't follow a scent over water.'

'Yes. I know what you've always thought, Bland. And I'm inclined to agree with you. But there's absolutely no motive, you know. Not an iota of motive.'

'The motive may be out in the islands.'

'Meaning that Hattie Stubbs knew something about De Sousa out there? I suppose that's reasonably possible, given her mentality. She was simple, everyone agrees on that. She might blurt out what she knew to anyone at any time. Is that the way you see it?'

'Something like that.'

'If so, he waited a long time before crossing the sea and doing something about it.'

'Well, sir, it's possible he didn't know what exactly had become of her. His own story was that he'd seen a piece in some society periodical about Nasse House, and its beautiful *châtelaine*. (Which I have always thought myself,' added Bland parenthetically, 'to be a silver thing with chains, and bits and pieces hung on it that people's grandmothers used to clip on their waistbands—and a good idea, too. Wouldn't be all these silly women for ever leaving their handbags around.) Seems, though, that in women's jargon *châtelaine* means mistress of a house. As I say, that's his story and maybe it's true enough, and he *didn't* know where she was or who she'd married until then.'

'But once he did know, he came across post-haste in a yacht in order to murder her? It's far-fetched, Bland, very far-fetched.'

'But it *could* be, sir.'

'And what on earth could the woman know?'

'Remember what she said to her husband. "*He kills people.*"'

'Murder remembered? From the time she was fifteen? And presumably only her word for it? Surely he'd be able to laugh that off?'

'We don't know the facts,' said Bland stubbornly. 'You know yourself, sir, how once one knows *who* did a thing, one can look for evidence *and* find it.'

'H'm. We've made inquiries about De Sousa—discreetly—through the usual channels—and got nowhere.'

'That's just why, sir, this funny old Belgian boy might have stumbled on something. He was in the house—that's the important thing. Lady Stubbs talked to him. Some of the random things she said may have come together in his mind and made sense. However that may be, he's been down in Nassecombe most of today.'

'And he rang you up to ask what kind of a yacht Etienne de Sousa had?'

'When he rang up the first time, yes. The second time was to ask me to arrange this meeting.'

'Well,' the chief constable looked at his watch, 'if he doesn't come within five minutes...'

But it was at that very moment that Hercule Poirot was shown in.

His appearance was not as immaculate as usual. His moustache was limp, affected by the damp Devon air, his patent-leather shoes were heavily coated with mud, he limped, and his hair was ruffled.

'Well, so here you are, M. Poirot.' The chief constable shook hands. 'We're all keyed up, on our toes, waiting to hear what you have to tell us.'

The words were faintly ironic, but Hercule Poirot, however damp physically, was in no mood to be damped mentally.

'I cannot imagine,' he said, 'how it was I did not see the truth before.'

The chief constable received this rather coldly.

'Are we to understand that you do see the truth now?'

'Yes, there are details—but the outline is clear.'

'We want more than an outline,' said the chief constable dryly. 'We want evidence. Have you got evidence, M. Poirot?'

'I can tell you where to find the evidence.'

Inspector Bland spoke. 'Such as?'

Poirot turned to him and asked a question.

'Etienne de Sousa has, I suppose, left the country?'

'Two weeks ago.' Bland added bitterly, 'It won't be easy to get him back.'

'He might be persuaded.'

'Persuaded? There's not sufficient evidence to warrant an extradition order, then?'

'It is not a question of an extradition order. If the facts are put to him—'

'But *what* facts, M. Poirot?' The chief constable spoke with some irritation. 'What *are* these facts you talk about so glibly?'

'The fact that Etienne de Sousa came here in a lavishly appointed luxury yacht showing that his family is rich, the

228

fact that old Merdell was Marlene Tucker's grandfather (which I did not know until today), the fact that Lady Stubbs was fond of wearing the coolie type of hat, the fact that Mrs Oliver, in spite of an unbridled and unreliable imagination, is, unrealized by herself, a very shrewd judge of character, the fact that Marlene Tucker had lipsticks and bottles of perfume hidden at the back of her bureau drawer, the fact that Miss Brewis maintains that it was Lady Stubbs who asked her to take a refreshment tray down to Marlene at the boathouse.'

'Facts?' The chief constable stared. 'You call those facts? But there's nothing new there.'

'You prefer evidence—definite evidence—such as—Lady Stubbs' body?'

Now it was Bland who stared.

'You have found Lady Stubbs' body?'

'Not actually found it—*but I know where it is hidden*. You shall go to the spot, and when you have found it, then—*then* you will have evidence—all the evidence you need. For only one person could have hidden it there.'

'And who's that?'

Hercule Poirot smiled—the contented smile of a cat who has lapped up a saucer of cream.

'The person it so often is,' he said softly; 'the *husband*. Sir George Stubbs killed his wife.'

'But that's impossible, M. Poirot. We *know* it's impossible.'

'Oh, no,' said Poirot, 'it is not impossible at all! Listen, and I will tell you.'

CHAPTER 20

Hercule Poirot paused a moment at the big wrought-iron gates. He looked ahead of him along the curving drive. The last of the golden-brown leaves fluttered down from the trees. The cyclamen were over.

Poirot sighed. He turned aside and rapped gently on the door of the little white pilastered lodge.

After a few moments' delay he heard footsteps inside, those slow hesitant footsteps. The door was opened by Mrs Folliat. He was not startled this time to see how old and frail she looked.

She said, 'M. Poirot? You again?'

'May I come in?'

'Of course.'

He followed her in.

She offered him tea which he refused. Then she asked in a quiet voice:

'Why have you come?'

'I think you can guess, Madame.'

Her answer was oblique.

'I am very tired,' she said.

'I know.' He went on, 'There have now been three deaths, Hattie Stubbs, Marlene Tucker, old Merdell.'

She said sharply:

'Merdell? That was an accident. He fell from the quay. He was very old, half-blind, and he'd been drinking in the pub.'

'It was not an accident. Merdell knew too much.'

'What did he know?'

'He recognized a face, or a way of walking, or a voice—something like that. I talked to him the day I first came down here. He told me then all about the Folliat family—about your father-in-law and your husband, and your sons who were killed in the war. Only—they were not *both* killed, were they? Your son Henry went down with his ship, but your second son, James, was not killed. He deserted. He was reported at first, perhaps, *Missing believed killed*, and later you told everyone that he *was* killed. It was nobody's business to disbelieve that statement. Why should they?'

Poirot paused and then went on:

'Do not imagine I have no sympathy for you, Madame. Life has been hard for you, I know. You can have had no real illusions about your younger son, but he *was* your son, and you loved him. You did all you could to give him a new life. You had the charge of a young girl, a subnormal but very rich girl. Oh yes, she was rich. You gave out that her parents had lost all their money, that she was poor, and that you had advised her to marry a rich man many years older than herself. Why should anybody disbelieve your story? Again, it was nobody's business. Her parents and near relatives had been killed. A firm of French lawyers in Paris acted as instructed by lawyers in San Miguel. On her marriage, she assumed control of her own fortune. She was, as you have told me, docile, affectionate, suggestible. Everything her husband asked her to sign, she signed. Securities were probably changed and re-sold many times, but in the end the desired financial result was reached. Sir George Stubbs, the new personality assumed by your son, became a rich man and his wife became a pauper. It is no legal offence to call yourself "sir" unless it is done to obtain money under false pretences. A title creates confidence—it suggests, if not birth, then certainly riches. So the rich Sir George Stubbs, older and changed in appearance and having grown a beard, bought Nasse House and came to live where he belonged, though he had not been there since he was a boy. There was nobody left after the devastation of war who was likely to have recognized him. But old Merdell did. He kept the knowledge to himself, but when he said to me slyly that there *would always be Folliats at Nasse House*, that was his own private joke.

'So all had turned out well, or so you thought. Your plan, I fully believe, stopped there. Your son had wealth, his ancestral home, and though his wife was subnormal she was a beautiful and docile girl, and you hoped he would be kind to her and that she would be happy.'

Mrs Folliat said in a low voice:

'That's how I thought it would be—I would look after Hattie and care for her. I never dreamed—'

'You never dreamed—and your son carefully did not tell you, that at the time of the marriage *he was already married*. Oh, yes—we have searched the records for what we knew must exist. Your son had married a girl in Trieste, a girl of the underground criminal world with whom he concealed himself after his desertion. She had no mind to be parted from him, nor for that matter had he any intention of being parted from her. He accepted the marriage with Hattie as a means to wealth, but in his own mind he knew from the beginning what he intended to do.'

'No, no, I do not believe that! I cannot believe it... It was that woman—that wicked creature.'

Poirot went on inexorably:

'He meant *murder*. Hattie had no relations, few friends. Immediately on their return to England, he brought her here. The servants hardly saw her that first evening, *and the woman they saw the next morning was not Hattie*, but his Italian wife made up as Hattie and behaving roughly much as Hattie behaved. And there again it might have ended. The false Hattie would have lived out her life as the real Hattie though doubtless her mental powers would have unexpectedly improved owing to what would vaguely be called "new treatment." The secretary, Miss Brewis, already realized that there was very little wrong with Lady Stubbs' mental processes.

'But then a totally unforeseen thing happened. A cousin of Hattie's wrote that he was coming to England on a yachting trip, and although that cousin had not seen her for many years, he would not be likely to be deceived by an impostor.

'It is odd,' said Poirot, breaking off his narrative, 'that though the thought did cross my mind that De Sousa might not be De Sousa, it never occurred to me that the truth lay the other way round—that is to say, that Hattie was not Hattie.'

He went on:

'There might have been several different ways of meeting that situation. Lady Stubbs could have avoided a meeting with a plea of illness, but if De Sousa remained long in England she could hardly have continued to avoid meeting him. And there was already another complication. Old Merdell, garrulous in his old age, used to chatter to his granddaughter. She was probably the only person who bothered to listen to him, and even she dismissed most of what he said because she thought him "batty." Nevertheless, some of the things he said about having seen "a woman's body in the woods," and "Sir George Stubbs being really Mr James" made sufficient impression on her to make her hint about them tentatively to Sir George. In doing so, of course, she signed her own death warrant. Sir George and his wife could take no chances of stories like that getting around. I imagine that he handed her out small sums of hush money, and proceeded to make his plans.

'They worked out their scheme very carefully. They already knew the date when De Sousa was due at Helmmouth. It coincided with the date fixed for the fête.

They arranged their plan so that Marlene should be killed and Lady Stubbs "disappear" in conditions which should throw vague suspicion on De Sousa. Hence the reference to his being a "wicked man" and the accusation: "he kills people." Lady Stubbs was to disappear permanently (possibly a conveniently unrecognizable body might be identified at some time by Sir George), and a new personality was to take her place. Actually, "Hattie" would merely resume her own Italian personality. All that was needed was for her to double the parts over a period of a little more than twenty-four hours. With the connivance of Sir George, this was easy. On the day I arrived, "Lady Stubbs" was supposed to have remained in her room until just before teatime. Nobody saw her there except Sir George. Actually, she slipped out, took a bus or a train to Exeter, and travelled from Exeter in the company of another girl student (several travel every day this time of year) to whom she confided her story of the friend who had eaten bad veal and ham pie. She arrives at the hostel, books her cubicle, and goes out to "*explore.*" By *tea time*, Lady Stubbs is in the drawing-room. After dinner, Lady Stubbs goes early to bed—but Miss Brewis caught a glimpse of her slipping out of the house a short while afterwards. She spends the night in the hostel, but is out early, and is back at Nasse as Lady Stubbs for breakfast. Again she spends a morning in her room with a "headache," and this time manages to stage an appearance as a "trespasser" rebuffed by Sir George from the window of his wife's room where he pretends to turn and speak to his wife inside that room.

The changes of costume were not difficult—shorts and an open shirt under one of the elaborate dresses that Lady Stubbs was fond of wearing. Heavy white make-up for Lady Stubbs with a big coolie hat to shade her face; a gay peasant scarf, sunburned complexion, and bronze-red curls for the Italian girl. No one would have dreamed that those two were the same woman.

'And so the final drama was staged. Just before four o'clock Lady Stubbs told Miss Brewis to take a tea-tray down to Marlene. That was because she was afraid such an idea might occur to Miss Brewis independently, and it would be fatal if Miss Brewis should inconveniently appear at the wrong moment. Perhaps, too, she had a malicious pleasure in arranging for Miss Brewis to be at the scene of the crime at approximately the time it was committed. Then, choosing her moment, she slipped into the empty fortune-telling tent, out through the back and into the summer-house in the shrubbery where she kept her hiker's rucksack with its change of costume. She slipped through the woods, called to Marlene to let her in, and strangled the unsuspecting girl then and there. The big coolie hat she threw into the river, then she changed into her hiker dress and make-up, packaged up her cyclamen georgette dress and high-heeled shoes in the rucksack—and presently an Italian student from the youth hostel joined her Dutch acquaintance at the shows on the lawn, and left with her by the local bus as planned. Where she is now I do not know. I suspect in Soho where she doubtless has underworld affiliations of her own nationality who can provide her with the necessary papers. In any case, it is not for an Italian girl that the police are looking, it is for Hattie Stubbs, simple, subnormal, exotic.

'But poor Hattie Stubbs is dead, as you yourself, Madame, know only too well. You revealed that knowledge when I spoke to you in the drawing-room on the day of the fête. The death of Marlene had been a bad shock to you—you had not had the least idea of what was planned; but you revealed very clearly, though I was dense enough not to see it at the time, that when you talked of "Hattie," you were talking of *two different people*—one a woman you disliked who would be "better dead," and against whom you warned me "not to believe a word she said"—the other a girl of whom you spoke in the past tense, and whom you defended with a warm affection. I think, Madame, that you were very fond of poor Hattie Stubbs...'

There was a long pause.

Mrs Folliat sat quite still in her chair. At last she roused herself and spoke. Her voice had the coldness of ice.

'Your whole story is quite fantastic, M. Poirot. I really think you must be mad... All this is entirely in your head, you have no evidence whatsoever.'

Poirot went across to one of the windows and opened it. 'Listen, Madame. What do you hear?'

'I am a little deaf... What should I hear?'

'*The blows of a pick axe...* They are breaking up the concrete foundation of the Folly... What a good place to bury a body—where a tree has been uprooted and the earth is already disturbed. A little later, to make all safe, concrete over the ground where the body lies, and, on the concrete, erect a Folly...' He added gently: 'Sir George's Folly... The Folly of the owner of Nasse House.'

A long shuddering sigh escaped Mrs Folliat.

'Such a beautiful place,' said Poirot. 'Only one thing evil... The man who owns it...'

'I know.' Her words came hoarsely. 'I have always known... Even as a child he frightened me... Ruthless... Without pity... And without conscience... But he was my son and I loved him... I should have spoken out after Hattie's death... But he was my son. How could *I* be the one to give him up? And so, because of my silence—that poor silly child was killed... And after her, dear old Merdell... Where would it have ended?'

'With a murderer it does not end,' said Poirot.

She bowed her head. For a moment or two she stayed so, her hands covering her eyes.

Then Mrs Folliat of Nasse House, daughter of a long line of brave men, drew herself erect. She looked straight at Poirot and her voice was formal and remote.

'Thank you, M. Poirot,' she said, 'for coming to tell me yourself of this. Will you leave me now? There are some things that one has to face quite alone...'

The
Agatha Christie
Collection

THE HERCULE POIROT MYSTERIES
Match your wits with the famous Belgian detective.

<table>
<tr><td>

The Mysterious Affair at Styles

The Murder on the Links

Poirot Investigates

The Murder of Roger Ackroyd

The Big Four

The Mystery of the Blue Train

Black Coffee

Peril at End House

Lord Edgware Dies

Murder on the Orient Express

Three Act Tragedy

Death in the Clouds

The ABC Murders

Murder in Mesopotamia

Cards on the Table

Murder in the Mews

Dumb Witness

Death on the Nile

Appointment With Death

Hercule Poirot's Christmas

</td><td>

Sad Cypress

One, Two, Buckle My Shoe

Evil Under the Sun

Five Little Pigs

The Hollow

The Labours of Hercules

Taken at the Flood

Mrs McGinty's Dead

After the Funeral

Hickory Dickory Dock

Dead Man's Folly

Cat Among the Pigeons

*The Adventure of the Christmas
Pudding*

The Clocks

Third Girl

Hallowe'en Party

Elephants Can Remember

Poirot's Early Cases

Curtain: Poirot's Last Case

</td></tr>
</table>

Find out all about the Queen of Crime
and her stories at **www.agathachristie.com**

Keep up to date with launches and news from the world
of Agatha Christie and discuss all things Agatha on the forum!

Shop online for books, audiobooks, DVDs and other merchandise

 /agathachristie   /officialagathachristie   /QueenofCrime

**For a touch of
Christie mystery,
scan the code!**

The

Agatha Christie

Collection

**Don't miss a single one of Agatha Christie's
classic novels and short story collections.**

The Man in the Brown Suit	*Death Comes as the End*
The Secret of Chimneys	*Sparkling Cyanide*
The Seven Dials Mystery	*Crooked House*
The Mysterious Mr Quin	*They Came to Baghdad*
The Sittaford Mystery	*Destination Unknown*
The Hound of Death	*Spider's Web*
The Listerdale Mystery	*The Unexpected Guest*
Why Didn't They Ask Evans?	*Ordeal by Innocence*
Parker Pyne Investigates	*The Pale Horse*
Murder Is Easy	*Endless Night*
And Then There Were None	*Passenger to Frankfurt*

COMING SEPTEMBER 2014

THE NEW *Agatha Christie*

HERCULE POIROT MYSTERY

BY SOPHIE HANNAH